Table of Co

The Vampire's Search For A Queen

Billionaire Fake Relationship Romance

By: Nikki Grey

Foreword

A fake relationship. I never thought I would be paid for that kind of work.

When you need money, you take what you can get. Being a bounty hunter isn't such a lucrative business anymore. It used to be. Now everyone thinks they know how to kill a vampire, which made vampires extra vigilant, and extra hard to kill. Thanks to amateurs.

The leader of a pack hires me to kill the leader of another. Weird, but OK. I'm in, as long as they pay well. But then, the billionaire vampire king himself offers me a better deal.

Be my queen. A fake one. Just keep me company and I'll protect you.

Sounds like a joke, right? Only, it's not. Especially when I start falling for him, and he starts thinking of me as his mate. This is where it all starts going to hell, as if it hasn't started that way already.

The Vampire's Search For A Queen

Chapter One

Irina

Killing vampire leaders is just like killing regular vampires. They only die a little more theatrically. Not that I mind. Garlic and crosses have gone out of style anyway, but silver bullets will always be your best friend.

These are more or less my thoughts, as I'm fighting my way through a crowd of vampires that are dancing to the sound of music I never understood. It is just noise, as if someone placed a speaker in a factory, then mixed all the noises from there together, creating some poor excuse for music. But that is what The Slaughterhouse club is all about. They sprinkle some blood over the heads of doped up vampires while some mind-numbing music is playing in the background, and you've got yourself a helluva good time. If you are a doped-up vampire, that is.

Which of course, I am not. Not by a long shot. I am still as human as they come, only slightly more dangerous for them than a regular old human. You see, I carry silver bullets, but I wouldn't waste a single one of those on any of these doped up fiends. They have no idea where they are or what they are doing. I'd be able to kill them easily with just a silver bladed knife. I wouldn't even need to waste any bullets.

I keep fighting my way through the crowd, elbowing left and right. Basically, just returning the favor. I keep hoping that the blood won't start spurting while I'm still on the dance floor.

"Woohoo!" I hear the crowd shout.

I close my eyes. Fucking hell.

Suddenly, the sprinklers open up from the ceiling and blood starts spurting everywhere. Fangs blast all around me, and if I weren't so calm and composed, I'd start slashing left and right immediately. I don't like fangs this close to my body.

I didn't think that my next target would be here, of all places, because he is the leader of a clan. Leaders don't usually party in places like The Slaughterhouse. Then again, leaders are different these days.

Just as I'm about to find my way to the bathroom, someone grabs me by the elbow, then the other, and I am lifted slightly into the air, hovering over the ground.

"What the hell?" I turn to my left, only to see a thug with those horrible nineties Diesel glasses that are all black. He doesn't say anything. I turn to my right side, and there is another one of those there as well. Together, they take me away from the blood, through a narrow hallway, all the way down the stairs, not letting go of me for a single second.

"Leave me alone, you pigs!" I shout, but they're squeezing me so hard that I barely stand any chance of wiggling out of their grip.

When we finally reach a door, they put me down, then knock on it. A moment later, the door opens, and I am pushed inside.

"I see you got caught in the blood rain," I hear someone talk to me, but I don't see them, whoever they are.

A lighter flicks in the darkness, illuminating only half of a face. And it is one of those faces you can't help but recognize. He inhales deeply, the bright red ember of his cigarette remaining the only light around him. I remain standing where I am. I'm a mess, that's for sure. My hair is falling in reddened whips around my face, and I can only imagine what my face looks like. I probably seem like someone who actually works at a slaughterhouse, which is a not very original wordplay on the club's name. I have to remember to tell Hannibal this when he actually shows himself in proper light.

"I don't like blood or rain," I tell him.

"I see," he replies, his voice oozing dominance, like a whip that is threatening to both punish you and caress you at the same time. I didn't believe when they told me that he sounded this sexy. Dammit, they were right.

Finally, he walks over to a small desk and turns on a lamp that, again, illuminates only a part of the room. My lips part in a silent gasp. Again, they told me he was devilishly handsome. They warned me, would be a better word. But I didn't believe them. How hot can a vampire be? Apparently, very hot.

His chiseled jaw is visible only from his side because of the light that is falling in that direction. He has a beard that seems both well formed and unkempt at the same time. His hair is swept to the side. He's got one hand in his pocket, while the other is holding the cigarette, which he keeps pulling at with his full lips.

For a moment, I truly regret having been caught in that stupid blood rain. If only I had arrived five minutes earlier, I would have been dry, and I wouldn't be standing here, looking like a butcher.

From the looks of it, he seems amused.

"Do you mind telling me why I'm here?" I wonder. He might have the upper hand when it comes to physical appearance here, but I'll lead this conversation.

He grins at me, showing me a row of pearly whites, with fangs that are barely even noticeable. "Do you mind telling me what a bounty hunter is doing in a vampire club?"

"If you plan on killing me, I won't make it easy on you," I tell him.

He chuckles. "I figured it was something like that." He pauses to take another puff of his cigarette, which he then extinguishes inside a crystal ashtray on the desk next to him. "But... to be quite honest, I had no intention of killing you. Unless that is, you force me to."

"Why would I force you to kill me?" I frown. "You're making no sense."

He chuckles again, deeper this time. His voice sounds like thunder from somewhere deep, underground. I try not to focus on it. It's too distracting.

"I actually have a proposal for you," he tells me.

"A proposal?" I echo his words, tilting my head, as if in an effort to see him better. But I can see him quite well. I wish he had kept it darker, to be honest. "What could a vampire possible propose to a bounty hunter that benefits them both?"

"I know of your newest contract," he continues, not paying attention to what I just said.

"How do you know?" My eyebrows knit.

My newest contract was supposed to be a private matter. A delicate affair. Only three people were supposed to be in on it. Now, the fucking billionaire vampire king, who has nothing in common with the guys who have hired me, has brought me to his office to offer me a deal. This day keeps getting weirder and weirder.

"It is... how should I put it... a matter of revenge, isn't it?"

"Revenge?" I repeat.

"Well, you were hired by the same vampire whose father you killed about five years ago," he tells me.

"How the hell do you know that?" I snarl. "I never share that info with anyone other than those closest to me and those who were actually involved in the kill."

"I know," he nods. "That is what makes you the best."

And still, the poorest. But I don't say this out loud. Instead, I allow him to continue.

"Aren't you afraid that when you kill one leader, your own contractor will deal with you?" he suddenly suggests an option that I haven't even considered. And dammit, it actually sounds plausible.

"I am not afraid of anyone," I say the first thing that comes to mind, but instead of sounding like a badass, I sound more like a spoiled brat.

"That is exactly why I wanted to offer you this deal," he continues calmly. I would have felt better if he got pissed or something. This calmness is too menacing. It is distracting me from the fact that I am stuck in an underground club filled with vampires.

"Offer me this deal so I can refuse it and go home to wash off this shit," I frown, looking down at the drying blood on my clothes and arms.

"It doesn't look half bad on you," he says.

Did he actually wink at me?

"The deal," I remind him. "Focus."

"It is hard to focus when I have a blood soaked human right in front of me."

"Then try harder."

He chuckles again. I try not to listen to that sound, which is caressing my ears at this point.

"The deal is quite simple," he finally says. "Your current contract is far too dangerous to consider. I can pay you double that. Triple, even. I can offer you protection as well."

"Who do I need to kill for that? The pope?" I wonder aloud.

He grins. "No one."

My eyes widen in surprise. "No one?"

"No one," he confirms. "Just pretend that you are my queen for a while. Spend time with me. And I will keep you protected and taken care of."

I look down at my blood-soaked self again, then back up at him. "Is this some kind of a joke you tell all the bounty hunters before you kill them?"

"You would be the first," he shakes his head. "But like I said, I would rather not kill you. I am beginning to find you rather amusing, even if blood-soaked."

"So, lemme get this straight," I point my finger at him. "You want to pay me to keep you company?"

"Sounds simple enough, doesn't it?"

"Nothing ever is," I shake my head. But I don't want to discuss this any longer. I don't like not knowing where I stand, and this offer certainly sounds like a joke.

"You do understand your position right now, don't you?" he grins, flashing those perfect teeth at me again. Only, I'm not sure if he's smiling or about to lick his lips, like animals do before they jump on their prey. "I could easily threaten you into doing what I want. Pretend that you are mine or I'll kill you. Would that work?"

I swallow heavily. I try to pretend that his words don't affect me. "I suppose that is how you always get your way."

"Not always," he corrects me. "But I could kill you. Be sure of that."

He takes a step closer to me. I don't back away. I stare him down.

"I'm too busy to look for a wife or a girlfriend," he explains in a voice that sounds more like a confession than a threat, but you never know with these kinds of people. Vampires, I mean. They lull you into a false sense of safety, then they slit your throat more easily. All I know is that I don't trust a single word he is saying.

"I need to show someone off," he shrugs.

"Why?" I frown. "Why is having someone so important?"

"It just is," he says in a tone that allows for no backtalk.

"Why me of all people?" I gesture at myself. "I mean... look at me."

"I am." His eyes flash as if lightning struck from somewhere deep inside of him, and the only proof of that was in his eyes.

"No," I shake my head. "I'm not doing it."

"Don't you need the money?" he reminds me.

Dammit. I do. More than I'm willing to admit. And the money I'm getting from the other contract won't be enough to cover all my debt that's been biting me in the ass.

"I can get money elsewhere," I snarl, realizing that he obviously thinks I'm for sale. Well, I'm not.

"Not this amount," he shakes his head. "And not with all the other perks I'm offering."

"I'm telling you that I– "

"Think about it," he interrupts me. "Then let me know."

Obviously, he's not used to people refusing him anything. And judging by the fact that he's not blackmailing me into this deal means that he really needs me. That is both thrilling and absolutely terrifying at the same time.

"OK," I tell him, then I point at the door, trying to find a way to end this conversation with me getting the upper hand. "I'll find my own way out."

That is exactly what I do, until I am out in the street, soaking wet. I'm starting to smell. I almost gag. I need to get home... fast.

As for his offer... he can find someone else to fuck around with. I've got work to do.

Chapter Two

Hannibal

It's been two days. Two whole days that Irina hasn't come with her response. It's not what I'm used to when offering a deal, especially a deal to a human.

I glance at my Rolex. It's almost noon. They should be back at any moment, unless there's been some unexpected delay. But they can handle it. I'm sure.

My cell rings, and I glance at the caller ID. It's someone unimportant, so I let it ring. That's not what I want to deal with right now. I'm waiting. Strangely, I'm waiting eagerly. I've cleared up my entire schedule for the morning, and–

A knock on the door interrupts my thoughts.

"Yes?" My eyes dart for the door, which opens momentarily.

My two right hand men appear, Mortar and Plyn. They are the ones who always handle my business when I'm too busy to handle it myself. This time, though, I didn't want to go myself. I wanted her brought to me, like the first time.

Plyn walks in second, holding Irina by the upper arm. She doesn't look happy about it. Her plump lips are locked in an expression of displeasure, and she's watching me underneath those dark eyelashes as if I'm about to bite her head off.

I nod to the guys, and they leave a moment later, closing the door behind them. She is standing in the middle of the room, where Plyn left her. Her nostrils are flaring at me. She's wearing a tight pair of jeans which frame her curves perfectly. I glance down quickly at her sandals with peeking toes.

Red nail polish. I manage to stifle a grin. Just the kind of color I'd connect with her.

Her white shirt is buttoned down to the soft line between her breasts, and there is a green pendant hanging around her neck. I wonder if the metal has absorbed the heat of her skin. Her shirt is slightly see through. I can almost trace a faint outline of her lacy bra, and it immediately makes me hard. I try not to think about it, but it's hard.

"Patience is not one of your virtues, is it?" She is the first one to speak, and her words immediately amuse me.

I get up from my leather chair and walk over to her. She doesn't budge a single inch, not taking those dark eyes off me. Everything about her is dark and mysterious. Maybe that's why I find her so alluring. Then again, it can't be only that. I've met many other women with similar physical features, and they didn't hold any power over me.

Not to say that she does. Because she doesn't. She is merely... amusing and alluring in more ways than any other woman I've met lately. That is why she is standing in my office right now.

"Drink?" I suggest, wondering whether to reply to her patience comment or not.

"No," she shakes her head. "I'm guessing that isn't why you told your goons to bring me here."

"That's true," I nod, shrugging and continuing towards the liquor cabinet where I proceed to pour myself a glass of scotch. I take my time, knowing that it's annoying her. Pissing her off, even.

Standing with my back turned to her, I know she's staring at me, all incredulous, drilling a hole in the back of my head, frustrated and angry. I let her simmer a little longer. I take a small, satisfied sip of my drink, and only then do I turn to face her again. I can see the annoyance in her eyes.

"I offered you a deal," I remind her, although I'm sure she doesn't need a reminder.

"I'm still thinking about it," she replies. I can hear hesitation in her voice.

"Your time is up," I tell her.

She lifts her eyebrow. "You told me to think about it."

"You had plenty of time to think about it," I point out.

She suddenly pouts. She does it so suddenly, then reverts back to an annoyed look. But it didn't escape my attention. Her lips became plumper, juicier for just a moment, then there was that guard again.

"To be honest, I don't know what's there to think about," I shrug, bringing the cup to my lips and taking another sip. She watches me do it, her eyes following my every move.

I remember that time I saw her fight. Those moves, that fire. Fighting her would probably be as exciting as fucking her.

"I pay you for your company," I repeat the conditions of my offer.

"See, that is what I don't get," she says, tilting her head a little as if to take a more scrutinous look at me.

"There is nothing to get," I tell her.

"Why would someone like you need to pay for the company of a woman?" she asks, sounding truly curious.

But this is not something that I'm willing to discuss, especially not with her.

"Why do you care what I spend my money on?" I ask, a little more seriously this time. "It is my money. I earned it with my own two hands and my own brain. No one gave it to me. Now, I want to pay you to provide a service. Isn't that what we use money for?"

Her lips part, but she says nothing. My words catch her off guard. I have an overwhelming need to grin at this silent victory, but once again, I resist the temptation. That wouldn't be a good start to this... business arrangement.

I know she needs the money. Everyone knows that. I could also easily threaten her into agreeing with this. But I want her to accept my deal out of her own accord. That's half the fun.

"All I have to do is spend time with you?" she suddenly asks. She's taken the bait. I can tell from the way she is looking at me.

"Yes."

This is a lie. But we'll cross that bridge when we get to it. I didn't get to where I am now by laying all my cards out in the open for everyone to see. That wouldn't give me any sort of an advantage.

"But what about my other contract?" she hesitates. She already sounds much more meek than she was a moment ago. Or it could just be a ruse, getting me to lower my guard.

"You have nothing to worry about," I assure her. "You'll move in with me. When you are not by my side, Mortar or Plyn, whom you've already met, will be by your side. You will be safe at any given point."

"Move in with you?" That seems to be the focal point of her interest, of all the things I've just said.

"Of course," I nod. "You'll be considered my queen by everyone. It wouldn't seem very plausible if we were living separately, now would it?"

With this said, I put down my glass, not taking my eyes off of her. Her back has arched. She is unconsciously trying to make herself appear to be bigger. She feels threatened, obviously. I'm just not exactly sure by what, me or the fact that she has to live with someone else.

"But... we weren't even dating," she points out. "And all of a sudden, I'm moving in with you?" She frowns. "No. That sounds implausible. We should have a period of dating first. I mean, pretend dating."

I grin as I walk closer to her. Now, my desk isn't separating us any longer. She is standing before me, so frail, yet stubborn. She knows she has to accept my deal, but she is still fighting it, for some reason, which is making it increasingly more amusing for me. Threatening her into it has completely evaporated from my mind. Now, my first victory will be in her yielding to my will.

"Well... what is dating?" I ask, as I stop in front of her.

We are so close that our hands are almost touching. I lower my head. She lifts her chin up only a little. Our eyes lock.

"What do you mean?" she wonders, sounding confused.

"Exactly what I asked. What is dating? What does it consist of?"

"Well..." She looks about, obviously welcoming the chance to look away and have a good reason for it. "Dating is when two people spend time together, learn things about each other, they share some physical contact, like kissing, holding hands. That sort of thing."

"I see," I nod, when she lifts her gaze to meet mine again.

Gently, I reach out for her hand and take it into mine. The touch is so sudden it makes her eyes widen in surprise, but she doesn't pull away. Instead, her lips part and that gives me the perfect chance to do what I've been planning on doing anyway. She merely provided a good opportunity for it now.

I cup her chin with my other hand, then press my lips against hers. I was planning on making it just a tender kiss, to prove a point that we spent time together, we kissed, so we could scratch the dating part off our list.

But her lips are so tender and juicy, I can't help myself. I slide my tongue through her lips unexpectedly, and instead of pulling away, I feel her intake a breath, then crash her tongue against mine with fervor I wasn't expecting. My body reacts to hers in the same way, our tongues twirling, wet and desirous, as if we're finally acting upon a wish that has been there all along, but neither side wished to acknowledge it.

Her fingers clench around mine, as my hand finds the small of her back, pulling her closer to me. The kiss deepens, becoming wetter, bolder. I expect her to touch me with her other hand, but she doesn't. Her mouth melts against mine, tasting like honey and I want more of it. But I quickly remind myself that this is just proving a point. Nothing else.

I pull away first, leaving her lips a little swollen and red. Her eyes flare up at me, but I'm guessing she's more upset with herself that she reacted like this, than at me for kissing her.

"There," I tell her, smiling. "We kissed. Before that we spent some time together. Technically, we could call all that dating."

Her brows knit in an effort to say something, but no words come out.

"I'll take your silence as a yes," I snicker. "Plyn will take you to your place, so you can grab all your stuff, and he'll drive you back to mine."

"Now?" she asks, shocked.

"Unless you have something urgent to do," I shrug, still amused.

"Well, no..." she tells me, all confused.

"In that case, we'll do it like that. Tonight will be your first night in my home."

"Just in your home?"

I almost chuckle out loud to her question. How naïve she sounds.

"Yes," I tell her. "I have taken the liberty of preparing the guest room for you. I think you will find it is most comfortable. Should you need anything else, you'll tell me tomorrow."

"Tomorrow?" she asks, almost like a kitten. "You won't be sleeping at home?"

At home. She is already making it sound good.

"I work til late, and yes, sometimes, I sleep at the office. I hope that won't happen tonight. But in any case, I'll be home late, while you're sleeping. I won't wake you."

It seems at that moment that she wants to ask me something, but she opts against it.

"OK," she just nods instead. "Let's do it like that."

I have to admit, I was expecting more of a rebellion, but her placid agreement has come as a pleasant surprise. I nod, mirroring her own gesture, then I call Plyn, who immediately comes for her, and within minutes, I am alone again.

Alone, and thinking about that kiss. I rub my chin pensively. I was merely proving a point. A point that this is just a business deal, on both ends.

With those thoughts in mind, I grab my cell and dial the last number.

Chapter Three

Irina

Sleeping is impossible. I knew that even before I put my head on this strange pillow that smells like fresh, new sheets that no one has slept on before. Even this whole apartment feels like no one lives here, but rather just habitates it, spending only as much time as necessary here. It should be a home, someone's home, Hannibal's home, but it somehow doesn't feel like that.

After what seems to be a small eternity of tossing and turning, I realize that I won't fall asleep. I check the small clock on the nightstand and see it's not even midnight. I doubt he's returned. I haven't heard the door unlock, though it's possible that it's not that loud.

I inhale deeply, sitting up in the bed. My stuff is still neatly arranged in the suitcase, lying open on the floor. I only took out my toothbrush and an oversized t-shirt to sleep in. The rest is left inside. I guess a part of me hopes that this won't last long enough for me to actually have to get cozy in this new place.

Unexpectedly, the memory of that kiss hits me like a ton of bricks. My cheeks flush a poppy red, which is something that never happens to me. I don't blush. No one has ever had such power over me, over my inner self. I swallow heavily, shaking my head at myself. I still have no idea how that happened. What on earth possessed me to kiss him back... like that? I seriously have no idea. It's almost as if that wasn't me at all, but some other, starved Irina.

Well, one thing is obvious. I need to have better control of myself when I am around him. That is all. Only... that seems easier said than done. Hannibal is used to getting his way in everything. Even now, with this deal, he convinced me. Honestly, the money convinced me. That, plus he said he would protect me. Going back on a contract is never a good idea, although I haven't taken any money from it. And Reyes isn't the kind of guy you can just back out of a deal with. Hannibal knows that.

Just a few days, I guess. Maybe a week... two? This can't last longer than that. I mean, seriously. I still can't figure out what exactly Hannibal wants from me. Just to play his little girlfriend? That seems preposterous, when he could just point to any woman, human or vampire, in a crowd, and she would be mesmerized by him, his good looks and his wealth.

I try to keep my focus on the money. That's a hefty sum, by any means. And the best part is that once I get my hands on it, I can leave all this behind, start a new life and maybe even open a little bakery. Yes, a tough bounty hunter wanting to open a bakery might sound silly, but I've always felt that this life chose me, instead of me choosing it. Situations forced me to react the way I did, one thing led to another and here I am now, sleeping in the apartment of the billionaire vampire king.

I push the covers away from my body. It's a hot night. And the memory of that kiss has made it even hotter, definitely something I wasn't looking for. I get up from the bed, and leave the guestroom, which could put any suite in the Ritz to shame with its fancy furniture, a Monet painting on the wall and golden faucets in the bathroom that is directly connected to the guestroom and can only be accessed from inside. I consider just stealing that painting, selling it on the black market and disappearing with the millions. But then, I'd have to live out the rest of my life looking behind my back. Hopefully, once I get my money, the other contract will expire, Reyes might forget all about it when he finds someone else, and I will be able to bake muffins for the rest of my life.

Again... I know it sounds ridiculous, but with all the excitement I've had in my life, I want some serenity. Muffins sound like just the right thing.

I smile at the thought as I walk down a hallway that seems endless. Strangely, it's devoid of any objects. I'd expect more showing off. Paintings, sculptures, any kind of obviously expensive art, but there's nothing. It's just a hallway, leading to other rooms.

Most of the doors are closed. Curiosity almost gets the best of me, but I don't push any of those doors open, to see what's inside. I'll wait for Hannibal to show me around.

To be honest, I have no idea what I'm even doing here, wandering around the apartment without him here. I was brought here by one of his thugs, who was surprisingly nice. I have to say I wasn't expecting that. I guess, I wasn't expecting many of the things that have happened, which led to me ending up here.

Finally, I stop before a door that is open. I've already realized that this apartment is huge. How could it not be, when the entire uppermost floor of this building is this one apartment?

I hesitate. Hannibal wouldn't want me to wander around by myself. That very thought ends up being the exact reason that I take that first step into this room. The entire wall is made up of one, enormous window, which is overlooking the entire city. Amazed, I walk over to it. The lights are mesmerizing. Looking at them from this perspective, it almost makes you feel like you own this city.

At least, Hannibal does.

I am here merely passing through. But I can't stop staring down below at the hustle and bustle. The city seems even more alive now than it does during the day. There is a small light in the corner of the room, and I find my way to it, illuminated by the lights from outside. I switch it on, immediately realizing that this has to be some sort of a living room. Only, there is no TV. Just rows and rows of bookshelves, all stacked up. There are several mustard colored armchairs, which stand in stark contrast to the fifties looking sofa, standing opposite them.

It is then that I see an old record player. I am immediately drawn to it, curious to see whether it works. It probably does. Hannibal doesn't seem to be the type that would keep something that isn't doing its job. Right by the record player, there is a stand, hiding what seems to be a million records.

My face lights up at finding Tina Turner. I almost chuckle out loud as I gently extract it from the others, holding it like a precious relic with my fingers. Simply The Best, Tina says. I always loved that song. It doesn't remind me of anything in particular. I don't connect it to any event in my life, good or bad. It's just, every time I heard it, it managed to make me smile. I don't know why.

I wonder if I could play it.

I look around, half expecting someone to jump at me from the shadows and scold me for not being in my room. But I know I'm alone. Besides, I won't play it loud. I just... need to hear something that will make me feel a little less stressed out than I am right now.

Led by a distant memory of how a record player works, I put the record softly in its place. That familiar crackling noise is heard, and the first beats of the song fill the air around me.

I call you, when I need you, my heart's on fire...

Without any warning, my body starts to move to the rhythm. Slowly at first, then it picks up. My hips sway to the sides, and I close my eyes.

You come to me, come to me, wild and wild...

Goosebumps start running up and down my body, which can't be held by the confines of this apartment. I feel like I am no longer here, where I don't want to be. I am somewhere else, somewhere far, far away, and I know exactly where I am going.

When you come to me... give me everything I need...

I lift my arms up in the air, swaying them, as my body swirls about. I am smiling as I listen to Tina sing, and finally the chorus blasts off.

You're simply the best...

I curl my fingers into a fist and put them in front of my lips like a microphone. This is where I can never stay silent. But I try not to be too loud as I'm singing. My eyes are still closed. I'm standing in one place as I'm dancing and singing, not wanting to slam my foot or hand or head against the sofa or the shelves. But being in one place doesn't diminish my joy at finding my favorite song among his records.

I know that being here probably isn't the best idea. Maybe I shouldn't have accepted Hannibal's offer. Maybe I should have just gone with Reyes. But none of that matters. None of that exists in my brain right now. I am filled with a sense of calm, ease that can only arise out of some distant memory that you aren't even consciously aware of, but it is still there in your mind. Or perhaps, it is a memory of an event yet to come...

Each time you leave me I start losing control,

You're walking away with my heart and my soul...

I can feel you even when I'm alone, oh baby don't –

¬This is where I open my eyes, my lips parted as I try to sing the final part, but no words come to me, as I see him standing in the doorway, leaning against it, all nonchalant, hands crossed at his chest... just watching.

When he realizes that I've seen him, he grins at me.

"Oh, don't stop on my account," he says. "You seem to be having so much fun."

Chapter Four

Hannibal

I never thought watching a woman dance in my apartment would be this erotic. She didn't even notice me for a whole minute, with her back turned to me, her eyes closed and her arms up in the air, swaying to the music. As she does this, her oversized t-shirt lifts up just enough for her underwear to show, a dainty pink.

I almost chuckle out loud. I never expected her to have pink underwear. Black, red, something like that. Not pink.

She is so lost in the moment that I feel like it would be sacrilege to call out to her. Besides, I'm enjoying the view too much.

Her charcoal black hair is flowing down her back. Every time I saw her, she had it in a ponytail. When she finally turns to me, I can't help but comment.

She of course, stops immediately, the song still playing in the background.

"How long have you been standing there?" she asks, instead of a reply.

"Long enough to realize how much you like this song," I smirk.

"Not only do you force me to come live with you, but you also make fun of your guest," she pouts. "Way to go."

"Is my guest hungry?" I ask, smiling this time. She isn't upset. At least, not as much as she would like to be. I see it as my chance to talk to her.

"It's past midnight," she points out.

"So?" I shrug. "I eat when I'm hungry. Don't you?"

"I usually sleep at this time," she replies, lifting the tonearm of the record player and stopping the music.

"The room isn't to your liking?" I ask.

Her eyes lock with mine, a darkness that I never even knew existed in them reveals itself to me. I wonder what she is hiding behind them. A part of me wants to find out all there is to know about her, her dreams, her wishes, her secrets. But I also know that it probably wouldn't lead to anything good. It would lead me in the direction where I never want to go again. That was the point of this deal. To get what I want without giving as much as is necessary on my part.

"It is," she nods. "I just find it difficult to sleep in a new place, especially the first night."

I want to tell her that I understand, but before I do, I realize something. We're not just talking here. She is opening up. Slowly, very slowly, but still. It was a good strategy, it seems, not to threaten her into this deal.

"If you're not hungry, why don't you come to the kitchen to keep me company?" I suggest. "I'm also not that hungry, but I haven't eaten in twelve hours. If I fall asleep with an empty stomach now, I feel like I'll wake up with a gaping hole."

"Twelve hours?" she gasps.

"The perks of being the boss," I smirk.

"Doesn't seem like perks to me," she shrugs, then walks over to me and stops right in front. "Well?"

"Well, what?" I ask, feeling like she is trying to regain control of this conversation, and she might manage to do it, if I'm not careful enough.

"Are we going to the kitchen?" she asks, staring me down. "I still don't know where it is. Plyn only showed me to my room."

"As he was supposed to," I nod. "I wanted to show you everything else. Let's start with the kitchen."

I turn around and walk out, not waiting to see whether she is following. I enter the kitchen, not stopping by any of the other doors, whether open or closed. I turn on the light, and it spills all around the green kitchen cupboards and cabinets.

"Green?" she says with a smile.

"Yes, why?" I smile back, walking around the kitchen island over to the fridge.

"I don't know," she gives a half-shrug. "It doesn't seem like a color someone like you would choose for a kitchen."

"Why not?" I chuckle out loud this time, opening the fridge and getting out some hummus.

"It's not... fancy enough," she says with an unapologetic grin. "It should be black or white, shiny and polished to perfection."

"I don't like shiny things," I shake my head, getting the bread out of the bread box, then two plates and a knife. I take those to the table in the corner.

"Really?" she frowns. She doesn't follow me to the table, but instead remains at a safe distance, as if she's afraid that I might decide to kiss her again. She is safe, at least for the time being.

"Shiny things are made to look nice," I tell her as simply as I can think of. "Practicality usually suffers. I like practical things. If they happen to be pretty at the same time, all the better."

This time, she smiles. She seems to like my explanation. She hesitates for a moment, then walks over to the table and sits down. She bends her left knee, bringing it to the level of her chin, resting her heel on the chair, like some rebellious schoolgirl.

"You want some?" I ask, gesturing at the bread and hummus.

She frowns again. "I thought you'd be fetching the caviar out of your fridge or something."

I laugh loudly this time. "Sorry to disappoint you. But I could get the caviar from the fridge, if that's what you feel like having."

"No," she shakes her head, trying to suppress a smile. But the smile eventually wins, illuminating her entire face.

"I like having a light snack this late," I explain, thinking that food was probably the last thing I would think that we'd discuss on her first night here. But it feels strangely pleasant. Strangely and dangerously pleasant. I continue quickly, and a little more formally than I intended to. "I can show you around the whole place, just after a few bites."

"It's OK, no rush," she tells me. "I can't sleep anyway."

"So, you like Tina?" I ask, taking a first bite of my bread with hummus.

She seems surprised by the question, then nods. "I think that is obvious."

I can't help but chuckle. "I meant to knock or call out to you. But you were so into it."

"Yeah," she smiles, raking her fingers through her long, luscious hair, pushing it backwards, away from her forehead. A few rebellious strands fall right back where they were, giving her that fresh out of bed glow. "I guess I should ask you the same thing, though."

This time, it's my turn to be surprised. I wasn't expecting her to ask me about music tastes that aren't mine. I swallow heavily before replying. "Not all of those records are actually mine."

"Oh," she replies immediately.

I'm not sure what exactly that means, but I'm glad that she doesn't want to discuss it in more detail. To be honest, I wasn't expecting to find her in that room, of all the rooms in my place. It's the room that has many memories, a room that I have to be in a particular mood to go into.

"Your place is really nice," she says, and it sounds like one of those stock sayings you tell someone when you don't know what else to say.

I nod instead of a reply, because I'm chewing.

"But I still don't get why I'm here," she adds.

"That again?" I wonder, finishing the last bite. "I told you."

"I still don't get it," she admits. "I don't like it when I don't get something."

"I bet," I chuckle. "All you need to know is that you are safe here."

"From whom?" she asks, tilting her head a little as she's taking a closer look at me. "Reyes or you?"

I stare right back at her. "That depends on who you consider the bigger threat."

Her lips pout just a little, barely noticeably. I'm trying to read through her facial expression, but it's hard. It seems that she has become just as proficient at hiding her true self as I have. This should keep me on guard. But instead, it is making me more and more curious about her.

"I consider the whole world a threat," she finally tells me.

"That's no way to live," I point out.

"If you've done it as long as I have, you get used to it," she says more indifferently than I expected. Or maybe it was just for show. At this point, I still can't tell.

I know many things about her. I know that she was left orphaned at a very young age, but still too old to be considered for adoption. An old woman took her in, when no one else wanted her, and that was where her life as a bounty hunter started. That woman, by the name of Maria Ortega, taught her everything, passing down the bounty hunting trade to the only person she could consider an heir. And Irina's subsequent life was filled with blood and money. Too much of the first, and too little of the second.

That is all my private investigator managed to find out. This doesn't mean that there wasn't anything to find out. On the contrary, that means that Irina has done a damn good job at hiding what she did not want others to find out.

"What do you need the money for?" I ask, and I know that I'm close to crossing the line right off the bat.

We're not friends. We're barely acquaintances. I almost blackmailed her into coming here and pretending to be my queen, and yet, the question slid off of my tongue as if it were the most natural thing to ask.

Her brows knit in surprise. She wasn't expecting to be asked this. I also wasn't expecting to ask her, but now there's no taking it back.

"What does anyone need money for?" she asks me instead of a reply.

"Do you always answer a question with another question?" I ask, trying to lighten up the mood.

"Only when I'm in no particular mood to talk," she explains.

She doesn't sound offended, but she is obviously pulling back.

"I didn't mean to pry," I explain.

"You mean, this is your idea of small talk?" she teases. There is a glimmer of a smile, which she isn't letting show. "I see now why you have to pay for a woman to spend time with you."

The animal roars inside of me in reply, but I immediately realize that she is still teasing me. Maybe this night won't be a waste after all.

"Am I that rusty?" I ask, snickering.

"Well, you're not smooth either," she chuckles. "Come." She gets up, heading for the door. "Show me the rest of your place."

A moment later, I do exactly as she tells me. I take her through each and every room, not really talking much because the purpose of all the rooms is pretty self-explanatory.

"You can go anywhere," I tell her once the viewing is done, "just not in my study. I don't like people in there when I'm not around. It's nothing personal."

"Sure," she nods. "You'll have your privacy."

"You'll have yours as well," I assure her.

She looks at me as if she doesn't really trust me fully on that one, but she doesn't say anything. I look at my Rolex. Now, it is showing 3 am.

"Maybe we should call it a night," I suggest.

"Mhm," she nods.

“Feel free to sleep in,” I tell her. “I have an early meeting at the office, so I’m guessing I’ll leave while you’re still sleeping.”

“OK,” she nods again, not offering anything else in return.

I walk her to the door of the guestroom. She stops, turning to me. I don’t know what I’m expecting her to say. Nothing, really.

“Goodnight,” she opts for the more logical thing.

“Yes, goodnight,” I reply, turning around and listening to the sound of her closing the door.

I walk to my bedroom, wondering whether all this was truly a good idea.

Chapter Five

Irina

When I wake up that morning, I realize it's almost noon. I guess I did manage to sleep well in a new bed, in a new apartment. I stretch with a satisfied yawn, glancing at the window. The curtains are half-drawn, allowing enough sunlight to illuminate the entire room, and now, it looks as if the finest layer of golden sand has fallen over every surface within.

I remember Hannibal's words from last night, that he won't be here when I wake up. I get up and take a brisk walk through the apartment, which looks slightly different now in broad daylight. It looks much more grand, more beautiful. Almost homey.

I stop in the middle of the hallway, listening. I'm not really sure what I'm expecting to hear, but there is no sound, other than my own breathing. I inhale deeply, then exhale slowly, relaxing myself. I continue walking in the direction of the living room, and the first thing I notice is a red cocktail dress lying prostrate on the sofa, straightened to perfection, although the shape underneath is doing its best to crumple it.

I frown in surprise, nearing it. Only then do I realize that there is a pair of shoes on the floor, and right by the dress, a note. Unable to stop smiling, I take the note and read it silently.

I was thinking we could have dinner tonight. Wear this. The driver will pick you up at 7. H.

I read it again, feeling my throat getting parched. I feel giddy, something that isn't characteristic for me at all, but it's a feeling I can't deny, nonetheless. I try to suppress this smile that lingers on my lips, but it's impossible, as I pick up the dress to take a closer look at it.

"Well, look at that," I say loudly, shaking my head. "The bastard knows my size."

It's still morning, and there's too many hours until seven, but I can't wait to try it on. I do so immediately, and a minute later, I am circling around my own axis in front of the big mirror in my room. To say that the dress is a perfect fit would be an understatement. There are no words to describe the soft, silky fabric that it's made of and the way it not only hugs my curves perfectly, but also falls down to the floor in a watery fashion. Reluctantly, I take it off and place it back where I found it.

I spend the rest of the day in anticipation of seven o'clock, rummaging through Hannibal's library, taking a long bubble bath, watching a movie on his huge TV. Somehow, the hours pass by without me even noticing it, and at seven o'clock sharp, the driver drops me off in front of a restaurant.

As I'm getting out of the car, I wonder if I should just go ahead and walk in, saying to the hostess that I have a reservation, then mention Hannibal's name, but before I can decide what my next step should be, I feel someone's hand on the lower of my back.

My first instinct is to turn around and smack them in the face, but I control the urge, because the very next moment, our eyes lock and his smile immediately disarms me.

He looks even more gorgeous than usual. He is wearing a white shirt, with the top two buttons left undone. His blazer is the same color as his pants, a royal blue. His beard looks trimmed, and he smells so good that it makes my knees weak.

"You haven't been waiting long, have you?" he asks, leaning in for a kiss on the cheek, which I allow, but I don't kiss him back. I suppose he expected me to, but I'm still getting used to all this.

"No, I just arrived," I tell him.

"Good," he flashes a row of pearly whites to die for, then leads me inside. His touch is electric. I know I should wiggle out of his grasp, but I don't. Then, he asks, "Shall we?"

We head straight for the hostess, whose red rouged lips widen into an astonishing smile upon seeing him.

"Mr. Delacruz," she addresses him with a voice as sweet as honey, which I guess is how all women talk to him. "How nice to see you again."

"Victoria," he smiles back familiarly, and I instantly wonder if they slept together. It's the first thing that pops to mind.

I scold myself silently. I shouldn't be wondering about that. I shouldn't care at all. But the curiosity is eating me up alive. My mind's eye can already see them rolling under the sheets. I blink heavily a few times, trying to banish the image out of my mind.

"Irina?" I hear his voice bringing me back to the present moment, and I know I must have made a fool of myself. "Are you alright?"

"Yes," I nod quickly. "Just had something in my eye."

I glance at Victoria, who is looking back at me. Instantly, I know that she is wondering the same thing about me. I smile at her, trying to disarm her, to assure her that I'm not trying to step in on what is possibly her territory, then I remember that this is exactly what everyone will think I'm doing. Hannibal is taking me out, showing off his newest conquest. At least, that is what he wants everyone to think.

Victoria shows us to our table, which I can't help but notice is the best table in the house. As we're passing by, Hannibal nods at a few people, all the while, his hand never leaving the small of my back . I know I should be bothered by it, that he's showing such possession, but I'm not. I remind myself that this is what I agreed to when I accepted the deal.

He pulls the chair out for me, and I sit down. A moment later, he does the same. The waiter appears out of nowhere, takes our order, then leaves again. The place is packed, and I feel like all eyes are on us. I guess that's what he wanted. That's why we are here, and somehow, I don't mind.

"That dress looks absolutely stunning on you," he says the moment our eyes lock. Something tells me he means it. It's not just a pick up line. There's no one to pick up. We both know why we are here. He doesn't need to compliment me. This is just a job, for both of us. At least, that is what it should be.

"Thank you," I say, mostly because that is what is expected of me. "You don't look bad yourself." This second line comes so unexpectedly that it surprises even me.

He grins. Obviously, he wasn't expecting it either, but he decides to go along with it. I'm not sure what else to say, so I welcome the waiter's arrival with our bottle of wine, which he proceeds to pour, after Hannibal assures him that there is no need to taste it first. He watches the waiter intently, then his eyes focus on me when we are once again left alone at our table.

He's looking at me almost as if he thinks I'm on the menu here, and I don't know what to make of it. That wasn't part of the deal. But I guess with Hannibal Delacruz, the deal is whatever he wants it to be. Well... not with me.

"You come here often?" The moment I say it out loud, I realize how silly that sounds, but at least I'm not thinking about the way he's looking at me. I'm thinking about my silly question.

He smiles before replying. "Only for special occasions."

I want to ask with special people, but I manage to bite my tongue in time before saying anything. I don't want him to think that I am interested in finding out anything about him, other than what is necessary for the deal we have.

"This is a special occasion?" This time, I don't manage to bite my tongue, I silently scold myself.

"Of course," he flashes me yet another of those picture-perfect pearly whites. I notice the fangs, barely there, but still visible, if you know where to look, almost like a tantalizing threat that at any given moment, he could sink those teeth into my neck and do whatever he wanted to me.

The image makes me excited for some reason. I banish the thought, but it does little to make that thrill disappear completely from my mind.

"To us," he says as he takes the wine glass in his hand and lifts it to me, not taking his eyes off of me.

"To us," I echo, clinking my glass against his. We both take a sip at the same time, and I realize that this is probably the best wine I ever tasted.

"Do you like it?" he asks, as if able to read my mind.

"Very much," I nod.

"It's an Argentinian malbec, from a little place known as Adrianna's Vineyard," he explains. "It is flavorfully dense, yet fresh. Can you taste all the layers?"

I accept the challenge, taking another sip. This time, I keep it in my mouth for a few moments longer. I'm no wine connoisseur, but I like to think that I would be able to taste a few well known things they put in wines.

"Are those... rose petals?" I ask, but as I say this aloud, I wonder if I'm just blurting silly guesses out. The look on his face assures me he's pleasantly surprised.

"Very good," he nods. "What else?"

I click my lips together, awakening the leftover aroma. He watches my mouth hungrily, that look again.

"It can't be," I frown, shaking my head.

"What can't?" he wonders, looking more amused than ever. His hand is on the table, his watch hidden underneath his shirt, only the outlines of it protruding from underneath.

"I think I can taste... well, not really taste, but smell... pine needles," I am still frowning as I speak.

This time, he chuckles out loud, leaning back into his chair. "I am amazed," he finally tells me.

"Did I guess it?" I ask, putting down the glass, realizing now how strong the wine is. His laughter sounds deeper, richer, more potent and more alluring. That is a dangerous combination.

"You did," he nods. "There are some spices and tobacco in there as well. But what you discovered were the initial layers. You have a good tongue."

He says it so mischievously that I almost blush again. Luckily, the waiter's arrival interrupts this conversation, and we both watch as the food is placed before us. It all looks tantalizing, and I realize how hungry I am.

He waits for me to start first, then we dig into our food, occasionally ceasing to chew so we could comment on how good the food is. I refuse a dessert afterwards, but he manages to convince me, and it is the best souffle I've ever had.

He takes care of the check, and on the way out, I can't help but notice Victoria's longing looks that she sends in his direction. The question whether they slept together pops up again, but even if they did, it is obvious that she was the one left hanging. He is now merely being polite, after everything. Or maybe, nothing happened, she just wanted it to.

"Shall we?" I hear him ask, and there is his hand again, possessively pressing against the small of my back.

"Yes," I nod with a smile, feeling slightly dizzy from the wine we had.

He leads me out of the restaurant and the fresh night air feels good. He suddenly stops me, then presses his open palm to my cheek.

"You're burning up," he tells me, sounding concerned.

"It's the wine," I explain, pulling back, as if his touch is the cause of this heat and not my cheek. But strangely, I want him to keep touching me. Every part of my body wants to be touched by him, devoured by him. "I think I had a bit too much."

"Let's take you home then," he says gently, lifting his hand, and a moment later, his car is brought to us.

Home. The word doesn't sit right by me, but I don't say anything. It is the only place where I can go now, the only place safe from the world... with him.

He opens the door for me, allowing me in. I slide onto the seat, with him following.

"Home," he instructs his driver, saying that word again.

Home. That is where I'm going.

Chapter Six

Hannibal

She falls asleep in the car, and I take her up to the apartment. I keep thinking that she might wake up at some point, but she seems to be in a deep sleep. I put her in bed, not taking the dress off of her, although at one point, I'm considering it. I'm considering more, but she's out like a light.

I tip toe out of the guestroom and go to the kitchen to pour myself another glass of wine. With the glass in my hand, I end up in the living room, slumped down on the sofa, with the small lamp turned on, shedding enough light to see the outlines of the objects and shapes around me. I down the wine in a few sips, putting the empty glass on the coffee table, then close my eyes. I don't know whether I fell asleep or I just had my eyes closed for a few moments, but her voice suddenly interrupts the silence around me.

"Hannibal?"

Her voice is soft, completely unlike her. She sounds a bit dazed. When I open my eyes, I see her walking towards me. She is still wearing that dress that looks like it was made with her in mind. Only, the hems have skirted upwards, revealing much more of her olive-skinned legs than before. I see her bunching up the fabric as she takes each step closer to me.

Her eyes look dreamy, as if she is still sleeping, and this is just some projection of her mind that has come to me. Her dark hair is falling in tresses over one shoulder, leaving the other side of the neck palpitatingly bare. The sight of it is enough to make my cock twitch with desire.

"What is it?" I ask, ready to get up, but instead, she comes closer, standing right in front of me now.

Instead of a reply, she lifts her dress over her thighs, up to her waist, revealing that she isn't wearing any underpants. Her soft, pink pussy is bare, revealed for me, and I all can do is stare at it in awe. I lift my gaze to meet hers. The desire in her eyes is palpable.

I reach for her, putting my hand on the back of her thigh and pulling her closer. This isn't what I was planning, not yet at least. But there's something about tonight that tells me this is a once in a lifetime chance. Neither of us was planning this, I'm sure. But the look in her eyes is pure fire. She is the dominant one now, although she is standing in front of me, naked from the waist down.

I lift her leg, bending it at the knee, so that her pussy is spread in front of me now. I bring my lips to her. She is soft and warm to the touch, as I spread her pussy lips with my tongue, licking all the way from her clit down. I hear her gasp silently, and a moment later, her fingers curl in my hair. I let her.

"I couldn't sleep," she moans, as I slide a single finger inside of her. She is already wet, begging me to fuck her.

Nothing in this evening pointed that it would end this way, but I'm not questioning it. I've wanted her since the moment I laid my eyes on her. And the animals inside of us must have recognized that same need, that same yearning and desire.

I grab both of her buttocks, lying back on the sofa and settling her right on my mouth, as I keep rolling my tongue back and forth over her sensitive clit. She's so wet, dripping onto my lips. My cock feels tight inside my pants, leaking. I ache to be inside of her, to spray her with my cum, but I have to be patient. This is already happening much faster than I thought it would. And both me and my cock are happy about it.

She grinds against my mouth, rocking her hips back and forth. My fingers grazes against that perfect spot inside of her, and I hear that sweet gasp again. She is so wet, so ready. But I want to pleasure her first.

She tastes too delectable for me not to want her cum dripping down my tongue.

Slowly, I slide another finger inside of her. The grip of her fingers on my hair is getting harder with each lick. My cock feels aching, throbbing inside my pants. The sensation is beyond painful. All I want right now is to throw her on this sofa and fuck her brains out. That is what I would usually do. But seeing her walk over to me as she did... The sight of that pussy lit me on fire instantly.

I suck on her clit more fervently now. Her entire body is trembling. All it takes are a few hard, quick licks and she comes undone on top of me. I open my mouth, my tongue sliding into her, taking the place of my fingers. Her pussy juices coat my tongue, my lips, dripping down my chin. I soak up every single drop of her wet heat, feeling her body slowly unwind.

Without a word, she drops down onto the sofa next to me, lifting her ass up in the air, with her hands resting against the back of the sofa. I quickly stand up, blind with need. I shove my pants and boxers down. My cock springs out, thick and beading with precum. I feel like all she would need to do was just graze her fingers against it, and I would explode instantly. This has never happened before.

She puts her hands on her butt cheeks and spreads them apart, showing me her pink pussy, spread wide. It glistens with her juices still dripping out of her. I slide two fingers inside.

"You're so fucking wet..." I murmur hungrily. I don't know if it's the wine or whatever the hell it is that got us both so hot and bothered, but I don't care. We'll talk about whatever this is in the morning. Now... we fuck like animals.

I press my fingers against her clit, rubbing it, while I take my cock into my hand, jacking it off slowly, as I watch her pink pussy.

"Oh..." she moans loudly, as I use her pussy juices to make my cock more wet and I stroke it harder and harder.

She lets go of her butt, and her own hand slides down, between her legs. She is touching herself now, her fingers playing with herself. My jaw clenches at the sight. She is making it impossible for me not to cum, but I try my best.

I can't resist pressing the tip of my cock to the soft folds of her pussy lips. Her fingers are grazing against my wet cock gently. I groan loudly. I feel as if my heart isn't in my chest any longer. It's sunk all the way down to my cock, and that is where it's beating now, throbbing loudly, about to explode.

I could just sink into her so easily. My jaw clenches again. She pushes closer to me, and the tip of my cock slides into her wet pussy. I wasn't imagining it like this. I had other plans, I wanted to take things slow. But I can feel myself on the brink of orgasm, and I know I won't be able to control myself much longer.

I grab her waist and pull her closer to me. My cock slides inside of her, as I part her wet folds. I linger in her for a moment, then I want to pull back, but she doesn't let me. Her ass rocks down onto me, and I'm unable to escape her grip. Not that I would want to.

That surge of energy rushes through me again. It's more powerful than the first time I slid into her. My fingers grip at her sides, as if our lives depend on it. I'm moving slowly in and out. I don't dare move faster, because I might cum immediately. I want to make it last, at least a little while longer. The feeling of being inside of her is pure bliss.

I grab the base of my cock and hold it pointing at her tight little pussy. My balls feel so tight, ready to explode.

"Deeper..." I hear her say.

My mind is telling me to take it slower, to make it last, but it seems that she can see right through me. She knows. Our bodies are speaking the same language.

I shove all of my cock inside of her. It makes her moan loudly. I can see her fingers gripping at the sofa. She arches her back, making it easier for me to enter her from behind. The feeling is pure perfection.

I keep pumping her without control. The sensation is too intense. Her pussy tightens around my cock with each thrust. I can barely breathe, as a tidal wave of pleasure erupts inside my body, and I manage to take it out just in time to cum on her left butt cheek.

Her entire body is trembling, so I take her in my arms, then walk to my bedroom. The darkness in the apartment is complete, but there are enough strips of moonlight coming in through the windows for me to see that blissful smile on her face. Her eyes are half closed, her lips are slightly parted. She looks like she wants to say something, but she doesn't. The silence is complete, so is the feeling of surprise, of pleasure, of utter exhaustion.

Gently, I lay her on my bed. I unzip her dress and slide it down her body. As soon as she's freed from those constraints, she wraps herself in the sheets, and moments later, her breathing has become rhythmical and soft.

I rake my fingers through my hair, my cock still in a state of readiness, although I know we're done for the night. I have no idea how or what possessed her to come to me like that, but I'm not questioning anything. Tonight turned out to be much better than I could have ever hoped it would be.

Still grinning, I lie down next to her. I don't know if she expects me to hug her, but I don't. That wasn't part of the deal. We haven't discussed it that deeply, but she'll get the hang of it.

I don't do postcoital hugging and kissing.

I turn around to the other side, with my back to her, and let sleep wash over me. In fact, it hits me like a ton of bricks.

Chapter Seven

Irina

I open my eyes and it is still dark. I am aware of everything that's happened an hour, two hours, maybe three hours ago, and at the same time, it feels like the Irina that did all that was not me at all. I dare not move in the darkness. I can hear Hannibal's steady breathing, but I dare not move.

I linger there, in that big bed, where I never thought I would end up. That wasn't part of the deal. Actually, we never even spoke about the possibility of sleeping together.

It's all that fucking wine, I think to myself. It has to be it. If I hadn't drunk anything, I probably wouldn't have thrown myself at him the way I did.

Oh God. I close my eyes, shaking my head softly on the pillow. I can't believe I did that. I have no idea what on earth possessed me.

Jealousy? I remember the way Victoria was looking at him, and I have to admit. I was jealous. Even though there is not a single plausible reason for me to be jealous of anyone. I do not own Hannibal. We're not dating for real. This is just make believe, on his insistence, which I still don't understand.

I'm only here for the money. Nothing else.

Only, this seems more plausible in theory than in practice, especially taking into account the fact that I am lying next to this same man who is paying me to be his... date. I don't know how else to refer to it.

Suddenly, he murmurs something in his sleep. My ears prick up, in an effort to catch whatever it is he's saying, but it's nothing that makes any sense, just a weird jumble of words that mean nothing, after which he pulls the covers to himself and resumes that steady breathing.

I listen to the sound of silence as the rest of the world is sleeping. I should be sleeping as well, but instead, I am here.

I wonder at all the life choices that have brought me here. I never knew my dad. He died in a car accident when I was only two years old. I have no memories of him, other than what my mom told me, and my brain hungrily connected those retellings, framing them into false memories. But I don't mind.

Then, mom died as well. Fortunately, this time I was old enough to have memories of her. But not old enough to understand why she also had to be taken away from me. At eleven years of age, you know that people die. Sometimes, they die a meaningless death, where it all seems so random, just like her cancer. Why did she need to be the one to have it, she of all people? I kept asking myself that question over and over again, but no mater how many times I asked it, I still didn't get an answer. Eventually, I stopped asking. There was no point. It was just a waste of mental effort.

I still remember the faceless hospital room, the nameless nurses and doctors, how cold her hand was when I touched her for the last time. And finally, the sound of that beeping machine, which was no longer beeping, but rather just released one steady sound. Even before that dreadful sound, I knew.

I knew from the way her eyes lost their luster. I knew from the way she stopped squeezing me back. She had very little strength left by that point, that I could feel her hand in mine. At that moment, the hand that was in mine did not belong to her anymore. It was just an empty shell. My mother's soul had fled from that earthly case. It was no longer with me. All I could hope was that she was somewhere good, somewhere where she could look over me.

Then, hell started. I didn't even realize that things could actually become worse than they had been. Much worse.

I close my eyes as hard as I can, as if this way, the memories won't hurt me as much. I might blur them out of my mind somehow, only that's not how these things work. Whether you have your eyes closed or open, you can't escape from the confines of your mind.

So, they flood me, as always. The foster homes. The time a foster mom broke my arm because I took a cookie without asking. The time a foster dad thought it was alright to sneak into my room in the middle of the night. I was already sixteen by that time, and more than capable of defending myself. After all, I had been training at the local fight club for two years already. And I was damn good at it.

I will never forget that day, because it was one day of light in a million days of darkness. I was walking down the street aimlessly, waiting for it to get dark, because I didn't want to return to my current foster home yet. I noticed this fight club, and they had an open door event that afternoon.

I don't know why I walked in. I guess something was calling me, but I didn't know what exactly. I was drawn inside by some invisible force, and now, so many years later, I am glad that I was. This was where I met the woman who changed it all around for me. She taught me that just because I'm a girl, I didn't have to take anything from someone who was stronger or bigger than me. I could learn how to fight back. And so, I did.

Maria was the owner of that club, and also a teacher. In a way, she became another mother for me, because I did not have anyone. The people who took me in, every subsequent couple, only cared about the money, and not my wellbeing. That became clear early on. There was no one I could rely on, no one but myself. So, I took matters into my own hands and learned how to defend myself.

At first, I sucked. I got beaten up more times than I could count. Maria didn't go easy on me. She also didn't tell others to go easy on me, others who were just like me, who had nowhere else to go, no one else to rely on but themselves. They understood the struggle. They also understood, just like I did, that no one will cut you any slack. They hit you where it hurts the most, so you have to play the game by their own rules. You hit them back, when they least expect it, where they least expect it. That is the only way you can win.

Only later did I find out that she was the leader of a small group of bounty hunters. She would pick the best fighters from her club and offer them a place in the group. She found jobs for them, in return she took a small percentage, and the fighters would get to keep the rest.

I gladly accepted. It was the first time in a long while that I truly felt like I belonged somewhere. It was the closest thing I had to a family, and she treated us all like her children. But life taught me a valuable lesson early on. Good things in life never last too long. You have to cherish them while they last, otherwise the moment passes you by, and it's all over.

It was all over a few years later. Maria died. A vampire killed her. He chose not to drink her blood on purpose. It was some personal vendetta, something in her past that eventually caught up with her. We all knew that she went the way she would have wanted to: fighting.

I finally turn to Hannibal, only to see his back. I feel like it's me the one who's turned her back on what Maria taught me. I didn't fight Hannibal. I surrendered to what he wanted of me too easily. I agreed to that deal, and not only that, but I also feel like I'm falling under his spell, something I mustn't do, at any cost.

I know Hannibal's type. They're used to having what they want. And I played right into that trap by throwing myself at him. Strangely, I don't regret it. It's been a while since I slept with anyone, and it's not like I owe my loyalty to anyone but myself.

That is, at least, what I try to convince myself of, as I'm slowly trying to get out of the bed. What's done is done. I don't regret sleeping with him. But I know it mustn't happen again. His touch is too electric for me to be playing with it. It's like playing with fire. All I need is the money that he'll give me once this deal is over, and in the meantime, I won't allow him to look at me the way he looked at me during dinner a few hours ago.

I know how silly that sounds, as if I can control anything Hannibal does. I can barely control my lust when I'm around him, let alone something else. But I know that there are things that are always under my control. Always. It is me who decides how I react to those things. That is how I can switch positions on him and regain control. I just have to play the part of the pretend girlfriend, not the real one.

We'll consider this strike one. Just a small mistake that won't happen again. It's the wine. A little bit of that dress and the way he was looking at me. That's all. Nothing that I can't control if I put my mind to it.

There, I'm already sitting in the bed, with my feet planted firmly on the ground. I just need to tiptoe out of the room and go back to the safety of my room. The guestroom. Because that is what I am, just a guest in this home, and I will be gone very soon, with the only thing I need from him, and that's money.

I get up. The bed squeaks ever so slightly, and I immediately stop in midair, my butt hanging above the bed. I dare not move, checking to see whether he'll wake up. He stirs a little but goes back to sleep immediately.

Relieved, I straighten and slowly start walking towards the door. The carpet underneath my bare feet is absorbing any sound that my footsteps might make. I reach the door and stop one more time to listen. For a moment, I thought I heard something. Not a noise, but something that could resemble a muffled sound.

I pin it to the concerned state of my mind. It's probably something very loud outside, and the way the sound traveled upward, made it seem almost as if it's coming from inside the apartment.

I inhale deeply, feeling exhaustion wash over me once again, like before. I walk over to my room and put on my oversized t-shirt which serves as whatever I want it to serve at the moment. I welcome the soft sensation of the fabric as it slides down my naked body. I glance at the bed. It looks too inviting for me not to jump right in. I nestle under the covers, still feeling a little awkward about what happened, but I remember that tomorrow is another day. I will be one more day closer to my ultimate goal, and mistakes such as this one will not be allowed.

Eased into relaxation with those thoughts, I close my eyes and, at that very moment, an alarm blasts off. My eyes widen in shock. I throw the covers off of me, sitting upright, looking at the door, which I closed when I entered the room.

My heart is beating in my chest so wildly as if it's about to break free. I can barely breathe properly. I have no idea what's going on, but I dare not move.

Suddenly, the door bursts open, and Hannibal appears in all his naked glory, wearing just a pair of boxers, holding the door.

"Are you alright?" he asks, as breathless as I am, and all I can do is nod, unable to take my eyes off of him.

Chapter Eight

Hannibal

The first thing I do upon hearing the house alarm is run towards the guestroom. I know Irina has become a target the moment she agreed to this deal, and I know I made a vow to keep her safe. Yet, the sound of the alarm is proof that I'm not being true to my promise. Whether or not that was intentional, is irrelevant.

Still in a daze between sleep and wakefulness, I am led only by one instinct and that is to safeguard.

I barge into Irina's room without knocking, relieved to see her still in bed, her lower body covered, but her oversized t-shirt is hugging the soft curves of her breasts tenderly.

"I'm fine," she nods, answering my silent question, at the same time looking concerned.

"Stay here," I instruct. "Lock the door. Don't open it until I come back, got it?"

She can hear the tone of urgency in my voice and only manages to nod once again. I expect her to protest, to say something just to disagree, but there is none of that. I quickly close the door, lingering on for a few moments, listening to the sound of the key being turned in the lock.

I was wondering whether to keep her close, but I realize that having her by my side wouldn't be a good idea, if the intruder is still inside the apartment. There could also be more of them. It's best for her to stay behind locked doors until I can make sure that the place is safe.

The alarm is still blazing all around me, piercing through my ears. The call should come any moment. The security, calling to check whether everything is alright, but as of this moment, I don't know that yet.

I pass through the kitchen, grabbing one of the knives, just in case, as I head to the front door. I input the code and instantly, there is silence again. I check the front door only then, realizing that it was left open. Heat explodes inside my ears as I grab the door and pull it open, but all I see staring back at me is the empty hallway, leading to the elevators. The light is on, revealing the presence of no one. Whoever it was, already left.

A million thoughts race through my mind. It could be anyone. I have a million enemies. A vampire in my position has made many of those, on his way to the top. No matter how good and benevolent you think you are, you're always bound to step on some toes as you make your way. It's inevitable.

As the uncrowned king, I am even more prone to attacks from anyone who thinks that it's enough to simply kill me and take everything I have for their own. Of course, things aren't that cut and dried, but that doesn't prevent others from still trying.

I have so many scars to prove that I survived attacks on my life. Too many. And I know that they aren't all over and done with. As long as I am who I am, there will always be someone who thinks that I do not deserve what I have earned with my own two hands. There will always be someone who will think that it is more fair to snatch away from someone than to make it on one's own.

But this is no time to take a trip down memory lane. I can do that later, on my own time.

I grind my teeth as I close the door, breathing in slowly, then exhaling in an effort to calm myself. The phone rings and I rush to pick it up. The security company isn't very up to the task.

"Yes..." I reply. "This is Hannibal Delacruz... five, seven, nine, three, eight, one, eight." I tell them my personal number, and they thank me, wishing me a pleasant rest of the night. I don't want to discuss anything with them over the phone, especially not right now, but it's obvious that I need to pay more attention to security from now on.

I go back to make sure that the door is locked. I pull the safety chain, settling it into place, as I used to do before, when I couldn't yet rely on fancy security alarms. As it turns out, they aren't that good, for all the money you're paying them. I'll have to look into something better tomorrow, but for tonight, hopefully the adventure is finished.

It takes me about fifteen minutes to check all the rooms, the safe in my study, the one behind the bookshelf as well. It all looks untouched, almost as if someone broke in just to show me he could. For no other reason than to mess with me.

But I can't figure out why they would come in and do or take nothing. Perhaps I caught them just as they were entering, and the alarm frightened them off. That actually seems like the most likely thing that could have happened. Otherwise, they could have attacked me while I was sleeping. They could have robbed me blind.

The thought of this doesn't sit well with me at all. I'm not used to my home not being protected, especially when I pay a small fortune for it. But there is no point in dwelling on that now. I'll have to take care of it first thing tomorrow. For the time being, all I can do is offer Irina my protection and assure her that she is safe, although if I were her, I wouldn't trust me.

I go to Irina's room and knock gently. For some reason, I'm nervous. I can feel my palms getting clammy.

"It's me," I tell her.

It takes her a few moments to unlock the door and open it. Her eyes are wide, still concerned. Her hair is slightly disheveled, a few strands falling over her forehead. She looks so wild and beautiful.

"What happened?" she asks, her lips moving slowly, accentuating every word.

For a moment, I consider lying, not to worry her even more. But I don't want to. She doesn't deserve that. It's her life that is in danger. She needs to know that we need to be extra vigilant.

"Someone tried to break in," I tell her. Then, I add, for clarification. "Actually... I think someone did break in." Upon hearing that, her eyes widen in shock. I try to calm her down. "I checked everything, every single room. There's no one here."

"Did they take anything?" she asks.

"I don't think so," I shake my head.

"Then... why..." she starts, but a glimmer of recognition explodes inside those deep eyes, and I know instantly what she must be thinking.

"It doesn't mean that Reyes already sent someone for you," I explain.

"Yes, but you can't be sure he didn't," she replies. We both know she's right.

"Look," I say, raking my fingers through my hair. She's right. I promised her safety, and I failed on the first try. That wasn't part of the deal. "I don't know what happened. It's a state of the art security system. Obviously, it failed, if someone managed to crack it so easily."

"What if someone knew your code?" she wonders, sounding less concerned. At least that.

"No way," I shake my head assuredly. "Only the three of us know the code. Me, Mortar and Plyn."

"Maybe they– "

"No," I cut her off with a frown. "No."

She hesitates to continue. But I know that what she was about to say isn't true. I trust those two as much as I trust myself. They would never reveal the code to anyone. Never.

"Rest assured that I will take care of it," I tell her. "I know I haven't held up my end of the bargain, but I will."

She looks at me as if she doesn't fully believe me, and for some reason, it hits me more than I thought it would. I walk over to her.

She doesn't pull away. Her cheeks are slightly flushed. Her dark eyes are burning bright. Suddenly, the memory of what happened a few hours ago flashes before my eyes, and I am aroused even more than before.

I know I should back away from her. I shouldn't be this close, not when she already has such an effect on me. But I can't seem to pull away. She is drawing me in, with a powerful magnetic force which I can't fight. Not tonight.

"I have a safe house, just outside of town," I tell her, standing right in front of her. "If you want, I can take you there immediately. It'll take us about half an hour driving. No one knows about it. We could stay there until I sort out this security system."

She tilts her head as she looks at me. Her lips seem even fuller, and the need to kiss them is overpowering. I know I won't be able to fight it if I stay this close to her.

"Do you think they'll be back?" she asks. She wants the truth. That is all I can give her.

"Not tonight," I reply. "But next time they do, I will be ready."

Those words of reassurance linger in the air between us, which is thick with anticipation. I wait to see what her next words will be, whether she will tell me that she is going back to her room. I want to grab her, pull her closer to me, but something is preventing me from doing so. All I can do is just stare at her, as if she's this precious thing that has somehow fallen into my lap, without me knowing it.

"I..." she suddenly says, those lips rounding up to make that sound. I give her a moment, curious to hear what she has to say. Her eyes are focused on mine. Her entire body is leaning towards mine, as if it might crash into me any moment, expecting me to pull her up.

A few seconds pass by, and she still doesn't continue. I swallow heavily, knowing that I could cut the thread of this moment with just one word, with just one glance, by looking away from her, but I don't. I am mesmerized, and all I can do is just do the same thing she's done to me.

"I feel safe here," she suddenly finishes her thought, and that is where I lose all my control.

My lips come crashing down against hers. My hands are exploring the curves and hills of her body, all the while pulling her closer to me, as if just by standing next to me, she is keeping me alive.

She melts into me, her lips as sweet as nectar. I yearn to drink from them more and more, forgetting about everything else.

Chapter Nine

Irina

I sink into his lips, completely surrendering to the sensation. Somehow, I want him now even more than the first time, as if that first time wasn't meant to satiate the hunger, but only to make it even more tangible, even more irresistible and all I can do is just let go.

My mind reminds me of all the times I had sex before. Nothing could have come even close to this, to Hannibal with his strong arms and dark eyes that pierce right through my very defense.

While we are still kissing, he slides my panties to the side, his fingers diving right into my folds, spreading them. Pleasure washes over me instantly, even more than I can take. I was already left on the verge of wanting more after that first time, unwilling to admit it even to myself. But now, under the weight of his touch and kiss, my need is undeniable.

My whole body feels like I've somehow gained superpowers. My every sense is heightened to the brim. My fingers ache to touch him. His scent is too intense. I feel like I can hear the sounds he is making with his tongue, and when he's breathing.

Neither of us can control what is happening, and I know that's not a good thing. This is only my first night here. What the hell will happen later?

I don't know and I can't think about that right now, as pleasure sears right into my skin, branding me forever. He inches his finger into my soaking wet pussy, and all I can do is moan loudly in response to his touch. He is reading my body perfectly. I don't have to tell him anything. It's as if he's anticipating what I want, what I need, and he does exactly that.

He adds another finger, and an even greater tidal wave of pleasure rips right through me, piercing me through my very core. He is stretching me, my pussy is wet and accommodating around his fingers. The memory of his cock inside of me is enough to push me all the way to the brink of an orgasm.

I swallow heavily. The scent of desperate yearning is in the air. He bends his fingers inside of me at a perfect angle, forcing me to push against him, to grind for more sensation, although I can barely handle this now.

My fingers grip at his face, pulling him closer, as if he might stop kissing me while finger fucking me, and that would be the biggest tragedy in the world. I open my eyes, unable to look away. He's not kissing me anymore. He's staring back at me, with a wide grin.

His fingers dive more deeply into me, touching that perfect spot. I release a loud moan, realizing that we haven't even started fucking again, and I'm already dissolving right in his arms. My clit is swollen to the point of explosion, as his thumb makes perfect circles on it.

"Just let yourself go," he tells me in a voice that immediately sends me over the edge. Deep and dark, I get lost in his eyes, my hands leaning onto him for balance. I come completely undone, as fire explodes somewhere deep inside of me. He wraps his other hand around my waist, holding me up. My knees instantly turn to jelly, and he slowly leans me backwards onto the bed, with his fingers still inside of me, feeling the palpitations of my body.

A few moments pass by, and he withdraws his fingers from me. Greedily, I want more, but I am unable to say anything. I feel like I've lost my voice. All I can do is just feel what he is doing to me. He looks up and down my entire body, with that same insatiable hunger that I myself am feeling. That grin is still on his face, and all I want to do is get lost in those eyes.

He brings his fingers to my body and voraciously, I think about his fingers inside of me again. Only, he doesn't do that. He traces invisible lines on my body with the tips of his fingers. The sensation is pure torture. It tickles. It awakens all the senses. I never want him to stop. My flesh is so eager for his touch, for his tongue, for his mouth. I've never been this wild for any man. And I doubt I'll ever be again.

He seems more focused on my pleasure, and that is what surprises me the most. I wasn't expecting him to be such a generous lover. I expected him to be selfish, to just think of himself and his own instant gratification, but he managed to surprise me again, just like he did when he rushed into my room to see whether I was alright. I guess there is much more to Hannibal Delacruz than meets the eye.

He grabs my thigh and lifts it up, making me wrap my legs around his waist, as he's lying on top of me. I expect him to slide into me immediately, but instead, his mouth crashes against mine once again. The dance of our tongues is fervent and wild. I never even knew I had such passion in me.

I can feel his cock pressing against my pussy, but he doesn't put it in yet. He uses his hand while he's kissing me to lower my panties, then pulls my t-shirt over my head, leaving me completely naked. He adjusts himself once again between my legs, grabbing my ass underneath me. I can't control myself any longer. I want him inside of me, more than I wanted anything in my entire life.

I pull my lips away from his. "I want you..." I tell him, as I gaze into his eyes.

He grins. "What do you want me to do to you?"

Heat washes over my cheeks, but I feel no embarrassment. I'm way past that point. "I want you to fuck me, Hannibal," I hear myself say.

Instead of a reply, he thrusts forward, into me. I take him in, feeling my pussy get stretched with each inch that goes inside of me. The feeling is incredible. I wouldn't be able to describe it in mere words.

I'm soaking wet for him, coating his dick with my pussy juices as he slams into me. He goes in deeper and deeper with each thrust. I am completely overwhelmed by the sensation, but at the same time, it doesn't feel like just fucking. It feels like so much more, as he kisses me passionately.

My whole body trembles, as I lose control. Neither of us can remain silent. My moans are becoming louder and louder, and his breathing intensifies through the kisses. I feel like he's managed to open a door I never even knew existed within me, and I'm afraid that now, once the door has been opened, I won't be able to close it again.

The way he's touching me, kissing me, pleasuring me, has brought on a new recognition of freedom and desire, unlike anything I've ever known before. I have become an animal in his hands, as he keeps fucking me hard. All I can do is moan and beg for more.

Just when I think that I'm going to cum, he pulls away, leaving my mouth agape in shock and my pussy throbbing with desire. He turns me around, placing me on my stomach. He uses his knee to spread my legs apart, pinning my hands over my head, so that I'm lying now prostrate underneath him.

"You are so fucking gorgeous..." I hear him murmur right next to my ear.

His other hand traverses the distance from my back all the way down to my ass, his finger gliding along my still throbbing pussy, feeling how wet I am.

Instantly, his cock slides into me again, finding its rightful place. I close my eyes, surrendering to the sensation. I can barely feel the weight of his body on mine, although he is keeping me pinned down. We are closer than any two bodies could be physically.

His fucking only grows in intensity, the friction becoming unbearable. I can feel his balls hitting me as he enters me all the way. I cling to him desperately, so close to cumming. But at the same time, I want to prolong this moment, to make it last forever.

It takes only one more thrust, and the most intense orgasm ripples through my entire body. I tremble underneath him, lifting my ass towards his cock, so that he can enter me even more fully, as my pussy contracts around his cock, coating him with my pussy juices.

He slows down the rhythm, giving me a moment to regain my senses. I close my eyes, slumping my head into the pillow. I know he's probably as eager to finish, so I lift my ass towards him again, and he picks up the pace. Within seconds, he quickly pulls out, erupting his hot seed onto my butt again. I moan softly as he finishes, then rolls off of me, landing onto the bed.

We're both breathing heavily, unable to speak. Not that there is anything to say right now. I am enjoying the sound of silence, the heat that is emanating off of his body. He leans towards me, and wraps his arm around me, pulling me closer. I still don't know what to make of it. I don't know what to make of any of this, but right now, my mind is in a state of a blur. I can't think even if I wanted to.

I close my eyes, although with everything that's happened, I doubt I can fall asleep. Instead, I'm just relishing the peace, the state my body is in at the moment, that post-sex bliss when you can't imagine ever being happier or more satisfied.

Then suddenly, I remember that all this is temporary. It won't last forever. Heck, it won't last much longer either. I will get what I came here for, and then I will leave. A part of me doesn't like that idea at all.

I know why. It's just my hormones raging. Dopamine is surging through my veins, and I probably think that I'm in love with him. Of course, that isn't true. Sex is cunning that way. It makes you feel things that aren't truly real, things that don't exist in your mind or heart at all, but that good feeling has got you weak in the knees.

I dare not open my eyes for one single reason, and that is that I might actually agree that I'm in love with him, if I see his face. It's better not to see him. It's better to just enjoy this moment for what it is. Just sex. Nothing else.

And of course, I will leave. I am not here to stay. That wasn't part of the deal, nor would it ever be. I just needed to get laid. I got that.

Now I'm waiting for my cash, and I can get out of this town, and start a new life, the kind of life I always wanted for myself, but could never afford. Now, through some lucky coin toss of fate, I managed to get that chance, and I'm not about to waste it just because my heart might think it's in love with this guy whose sex skills are beyond amazing.

It's just a mixture of hormones which will dissipate in the morning.

Finally, with a blissed smile on my face, I manage to fall asleep. I don't dream. It's been a long time since I was able to dream of something nice, but at least, my slumber isn't plagued by nightmares. It was a restful sleep, the kind that makes you happy to be alive when you open your eyes.

Waking up without him was something I expected. He was already gone from my room, but I didn't mind. I went ahead and made myself some coffee, determined to enjoy this day, despite the fact that I had to stay inside, just in case. I could go out, but that would mean that I needed to be escorted by one of Hannibal's two right hand men.

I have the whole apartment at my disposal. Perhaps roaming Hannibal's apartment instead of roaming the city might prove to be more rewarding.

Chapter Ten

Hannibal

"Do you have any idea who it could be?" Everild asked, as we were sitting in my office.

It was still relatively early in the morning, a time when he knew I would be available for a catch up, as we haven't seen each other in a while. Although we have been best friends for years, we do not see each other as much as we would have liked to. Life has a way of keeping people apart, and some of them allow this distance to diminish the strength of their friendship. But not us.

Everild has been my best friend ever since I could remember. We shared the bad times, of which there were more than I would like to remember. But we're both capable, and quickly turned that around. He was there by my side during the most difficult times of my life, and that is something I will never forget.

"No idea," I shake my head, as I look at him.

As the leader of a vampire clan, he has gained not only quite a following, but also he has grown. Not physically, but rather mentally. Somehow, I see him as someone more than who he has been, and that is because of all the responsibilities that have been placed upon him. He isn't accountable solely for himself now, but for many others.

He always had that boyish charm about him, which made him appear like someone who might not be able to handle all the responsibilities that come with a certain age, with a certain position in life. He always had that tendency to go with the flow, while I was the one who liked to focus my direction, rather than have someone else, even fate, do it for me. That was always where we differed, and yet, at the same time, it seemed to make us even closer as friends, because we could understand the other's point of view.

"Nothing was taken?" he continues, leaning back in the chair. His dark hair stands in stark contrast with his sky blue eyes, which always seemed to manage to draw the truth out of someone, even without any force. He had a way of looking at you, of awakening trust in you, making you feel like he would understand you no matter what you were going through. He would make you open up to him, without even realizing it.

"Nothing of value at least," I shrug, getting up, feeling restless.

Now, I'm not sure if that restlessness is the result of the break in or something else. But I don't want to think about that now. Today, I have many business meetings lined up, and I also have to speak with the security company about the way they're handling business. Trying to figure out why I'm being so restless and whether it has anything to do with the woman in my apartment is not something I want to focus on right now.

"It's a good thing no one got hurt," he tells me, and I know he's right. It could have ended very badly.

"Do you know how that someone could have found out your code?" Everild asks me curiously.

"That is what I've been thinking as well," I nod. "I don't have it written down anywhere. And I'm completely assured that Plyn and Mortar kept their mouths shut."

Everild just nods back at me, his eyes focused on mine. I can see all the sympathy and understanding in them. As my best friend, perhaps he believes that he should also know the code. But I think three people knowing is more than enough.

In addition to this, I obviously need to change the code combination. It's the exact hours when Xeena turned into a vampire. I know it's the most pathetic choice, but now it serves as more than just a reminder of who I was and who I would never want to become ever again. Now, it's making me think that someone might have actually thought of it themselves.

I instructed Plyn to keep an eye on the apartment while I'm gone, but I doubt that whoever had the balls to break in last night would be brave enough to do it in broad daylight. And by tonight, we'll be ready for them.

"I guess it's something to be expected," I shrug, staring out of the window, which overlooks the entire city.

It belongs to me. All of it. I am the unnamed king of everything I see. Of course, it is to be expected that someone will try to take it away from me. But I thought I was better prepared. That is the thing that caught me off guard, especially now that I have someone to protect.

"So... who's the girl?" Everild asks, and I realize now that this deal with Irina happened so quickly and so unexpectedly that I didn't even have any time to share it with my best friend.

I turn to face him once again. There is a wide grin on my face.

"I can't remember the last time I saw you grinning like that about a girl," Everild comments.

I quickly bring him up to date on what happened in the last couple of days, when he cuts me off.

"Wait," he says. "Are you talking about the bounty hunter Reyes hired?"

"Yes," I nod. "That's exactly her."

"So, their deal is off?" he wonders, with an undertone of worry.

"Yes," I repeat.

"Well..." he sighs, raking his fingers through his charcoal black hair. "You know he won't like that."

I frown. "And I care about what he likes?"

"No," he shrugs. "But you know he's a nasty piece of work when he doesn't get what he wants."

"That I know," I agree. "That is why I need to keep Irina safe, at my place."

"But wait..." Everild lifts his hands at the level of his chest, showing me that he isn't quite clear on the rules of this deal I have with her. "You guys are really together?"

"No," I shake my head. "Not technically. I want her to pretend to be my girlfriend, because some of the other leaders have expressed their concerns about my legacy and whether there will be any."

Everild frowns. "But that's your own business."

"Not when you're king," I remind him. "They need to know that there will be someone to carry on my name, and to tell you honestly, I'm tired of trying to find someone."

The truth is that I haven't really been trying to find anyone. All I ever needed was to forget my current worries in someone's arms for the night. That was enough. But none of us is getting any younger, and I've realized that the only way to obtain what I want would be to pay for it. Although that sounds horrible by any standards, it's actually the cleanest option. Both sides agree to get exactly what is stated, no more, no less. No hurt feelings, no expectations that can't be met.

I know I haven't really revealed my entire plan to Irina, but hopefully, she will agree to it. The point isn't just to assure everyone that I have found someone to spend the rest of my life with, but to show them that I am well on my way to creating my legacy, which is what I truly want to do.

As for Irina's presence in my life, in those kids' lives... that is yet to be determined how it will function. Neither of us wants to be together. That much is clear. The sex is fantastic, but that is just sex. Those things fizzle quickly, as I've witnessed so many times. What I need from her is to provide me with offspring, but without the added element of a romantic relationship.

"I'm not interested in a relationship, Everild, you know this," I tell him.

"I thought you would eventually change your mind."

"I didn't. And I won't," I say.

This is a topic that we've discussed many times before, especially after the time when Xeena left, taking everything of mine with her. My heart, my pride, my dignity. It took me a long time to get all those things back, and now I am reluctant to ever part with them again.

"You think Irina will agree to have kids with you but then not have a relationship with you?" When that idea formed in my mind, it made sense. Now that I hear it said from his point of view, I realize that maybe women don't function like that. But I'm hoping that we will still be able to find some common ground, where we will both get what we want.

"She seems like a reasonable woman," I shrug. "That is partly why I chose her."

"A vampire chose a bounty hunter to prolong his legacy," Everild says it out loud again, and it sounds even more ridiculous now. He's suppressing a bout of laughter.

"I wanted a woman who could fight," I explain. "A woman with a spark in her. Not these pretty faces that are just empty shells of who they could be."

"Irina isn't just a pretty face," Everild points out. "Although I'm guessing her pretty face doesn't hurt."

"Not at all," I grin, instantly remembering how she closed her eyes, opened her pretty little mouth and dissolved with my cock inside of her. I have never seen a more beautiful woman than she was at that moment. "But enough talk about women. Tell me what has been new with you? Have you spoken with the elders lately?"

All the leaders of every single clan have to meet up occasionally with the elders, so that the peace between the clans can be kept up. Everild gives me a meaningful glance, and he knows instantly who I am referring to.

Reyes was responsible for the death of his father. Everyone knows this. But because of some loophole in the old laws, he managed to escape punishment. Also, he somehow convinced the elders that he had repented for all that, and he was now a changed vampire. As if such a thing could ever be.

Now, he has hired Irina to kill the newest leader of his clan, but that is also a well-kept secret. I doubt that more than five people know about it, including me and Irina. I know what he wants. He is hoping that by doing away with Almodovar, the current leader of his clan, he will be the next one in line. Not only that, but I also wouldn't be surprised if he was planning on screwing her over somehow. After all, she was the one who killed his father. Again, a secret that is well kept among the confines of the vampire community, but that piece of information could leak very easily, and Irina would be in even more trouble than she is right now.

"I have been busy with my own investments," Everild admits. "That is also why I am here. I need some business advice."

"You know I am always there for you, whatever you need," I assure him, sitting down at my desk. "Tell me what's on your mind."

We spend the next hour discussing his options, after which he leaves, and my day starts. One meeting follows another, and I can barely focus on them. I'm constantly wondering what Irina is up to.

When my third meeting for the day comes to an end, I check my watch. It's two pm. Maybe I could cancel the next meeting, go back home and have lunch with her. Just to make sure that she isn't worried and that everything is alright, of course. For no other reason than that. What other reason could there be?

Chapter Eleven

Irina

I know I shouldn't. My mind is telling me that some things should be left alone, especially when you are a guest in someone else's home.

I roam through the apartment and all the rooms, trying to avoid that one room that has captured my attention. Hannibal's study. That is the place where I can find out more about him than he wants me to know.

Why would you want to find out more about him?

That question appears in my mind so suddenly, so unexpectedly that I don't know how to answer it. My first response is, of course, I want to find out more about the man I share a home with currently. What if he is dangerous? What if he is not to be trusted? What if he has some terrible secret that is putting my life in danger just by being here?

Those are the thoughts that are swarming through my mind as I'm standing in front of the door to Hannibal's study. The door is closed, but something is telling me it's not locked. If it was, then it would be settled. I would be kept out, by forces that were not under my control and that would be that.

A part of me even wants it to be locked. I want to be kept away from this man, almost as much as I am drawn to him. There is an undeniable attraction between us, something I didn't anticipate. I thought this would be simply a job, just a means for me to get enough money so I could leave this bounty hunter lifestyle behind and start anew somewhere.

I could not have expected that I would fall for Hannibal. Yes, I said it. I feel like I maybe haven't fallen yet, but I'm surely slipping down that slope, with no means of stopping. And right now, I find myself standing in front of his study. That would be yet another downward slope, from which I know I will not return. What if I find out something about him, something that will seal the deal and I will never think of any other man but him?

I sigh deeply. I shouldn't think like that. I should keep my mind focused on the money. That is why I'm here. The sex is just... a bonus. If I keep this outlook, I will be home safe once this whole thing ends.

I hesitate to open the door. My hand is trembling. I know I shouldn't. I know I myself would be pissed if I welcomed someone into my home, and then caught them rummaging through my personal stuff, the same stuff that I want to keep hidden away from the rest of the world.

But he's not here, is he? The devil on my shoulder asks softly, whispering into my ear.

Yes, that is true. He isn't here. He probably won't be here for hours. I could just go inside, take a quick look, provided the door is unlocked, of course, and I could be out shortly. I would just have to make sure not to touch anything or move it, otherwise, he will notice. People like that notice everything.

People like that...like what? I realize that I know so little about him. All I know is what everyone else knows. This is the persona he himself has released into the world. But I know there must be more to who he is. That is the person I want to get to know.

Why?

That devil isn't making a whole lot of sense. First, it's urging me to go inside and discover all I can about this man, and now, when I'm wondering about him, that same devil is asking me why I am doing all this. I swear, the devil must be a woman. He has no idea what he wants, and neither do I.

Determined enough, I grab the doorknob and turn it, pushing the door open. My heart is beating like mad with fear, with excitement, with sheer curiosity. The end result is a strange mixture that is making me both stay put and urging me to turn around while I'm still relatively safe here. In this room, I might find out something that might change everything.

Still, despite this fear, I take a bold step inside, and instantly, the smell of smoky rich, aged Scotch hits my nostrils. There is something else in there, the fragrance of old books and worn-out leather. Immediately, a sense of calm washes over me, as if I've crossed over into some unknown territory, and even before I knew anything about it, my first instincts are telling me it's OK. I can relax. There is no danger here.

But I can't trust that feeling, just like I can't trust Hannibal. I feel like I can't trust any vampire, any more than I can trust any man. Life taught me that you can only rely on yourself. Everyone else can disappoint you, even after they've assured you that they have your best interests at heart. People lie. People and vampires alike. So, it's best to always keep looking behind your shoulder when dealing with both.

The first place I walk over to is his desk. I press my fingers against the hard, polished surface. It looks deeply worn-out, as if someone has been sitting at it for decades, lovingly writing, reading, pouring out his mind over it. I can imagine Hannibal doing exactly that.

I shake my head at myself. I still think this is wrong. But I'm already inside. Now, there would be no force on earth to drag me out of this place.

I walk around his desk, and sit in his chair, which squeaks lightly under the weight of my body. I feel a soft indentation where my whole self sinks into. The thought of his body having made that makes me feel... giddy.

I immediately frown as soon as my brain comes up with that word. I shouldn't feel giddy about anyone, especially not him.

I get up from the chair, still frowning at myself. I pace about the room slowly, feeling like I'm in some sacred place, which I should not disturb with my presence. I turn around and glance at the door, half-expecting to see Hannibal standing there.

Don't be silly, the devil says. He's still at work, and that's where he will be all day. He's a workaholic. You don't think that he'll just appear out of nowhere to spend time with you?

The tone inside my mind is mocking.

"I really have to stop having conversations with myself," I say out loud, just so I can balance everything out.

The bookshelf is the next thing that captures my attention. I walk over to it, stepping over the frayed, oriental carpet, which has a faded circle right in the middle, as if someone intentionally kept rubbing their feet there over and over again. Despite looking shabby, it does add to the general antique feel of the whole room. Everything seems old and worn, yet I doubt that there was any way in which this room could be more suited to the man using it.

I stand in front of the bookshelf, eyeing the titles. They are mostly classics, but some are rather obscure authors and book titles which I've never heard of, although I like to pride myself on having read many books. Then, I notice that there are other things on the bookshelf. I see a porcelain box with a lid. I open it, peering inside, only to find an unused candle. I inhale and the sweet scent of vanilla pierces through my nostrils. I make sure to put it back exactly where it was, with the flowers pointing towards the middle of the room.

All the way in the corner, there is a framed photograph of a woman. Her smile is mesmerizing. Her long, honey-colored hair is falling down both her shoulders, all the way down her red dress. Her eyes are wide, demanding focus even though it is only a photograph, and yet I feel like I can't look away. She is unlike any other woman I've ever seen before.

Instantly, the grip of the green-eyed monster clenches at me, and I can't deny its existence, no matter how much I'd like to. I take the frame in my hands, touching it only with the tips of my fingers, as if it would burn me if I touched it properly. I bring it closer to my field of vision, and upon closer inspection, the woman looks even more bewitching, as if there is some magic in those eyes, in that smile, in that porcelain white skin.

I wonder who she is.

Isn't it obvious?

I frown. It probably is. I want to consider other options as well. A sister, maybe? She can't be his daughter? Maybe... she could? How old are vampires, anyway? He could be ancient.

It's all a tangle of thoughts, as I try to come up with an alternative explanation as to who this woman might be, but there is only one. She has to be someone important, otherwise, why would he have her photo framed in his study? She must be the woman he loves... or loved, my mind silently adds.

No, if he loved her, she would be in a drawer somewhere. She is out, visible. Which must mean that he wants to keep looking at her.

I know I shouldn't care. But I can't stop looking at her, wondering what she meant to him, who she was to him. We all suffered heartbreak in our lives. That is inescapable. But the worst part is when you can't get over it, when this heartbreak from the past follows you into the present, determining your future. That is when you are stuck in a vicious cycle, unable to find your way out.

I stare at the smiling woman, wondering if that is what she is to Hannibal, a vicious cycle that has him stuck, spinning around and around, until the end of his days.

Suddenly, I hear the door unlock, and that sound makes me jerk unexpectedly. Instantly, I drop the frame down to the ground, onto the floorboards, where the carpet did not reach. The frame breaks, shattering the glass all around my bare feet. I dare not move, out of fear of stepping onto the broken glass, so I remain put, knowing that Hannibal will come here at any moment.

If that's him... At this point, a part of me almost wishes that whoever unlocked the door wasn't him, but rather the same person who tried to break in last night. I would be able to handle myself with an enemy. I would kick his ass, or at least try to. But if it's Hannibal... that would mean that he caught me doing something I wasn't supposed to be doing. I was snooping. And on top of that, I broke his frame.

I lift my gaze towards the door. Only now do I realize that he's standing there, staring at me, impassively.

I can't read him at all, and that is the most frightening thing. I don't know how angry he is with me. I want him to speak, but he doesn't. He is just staring me down in disbelief, as if I disappointed him beyond belief.

"I..." I say instead of him, but that is all I manage.

His gaze traverses the distance between my eyes, down to my bare feet and the shattered glass. Then, our eyes lock again.

"What have you done?" he finally asks, and all I can think is that I'm wondering this same thing myself.

Chapter Twelve

Hannibal

"I'm sorry, I..." she says, with a stutter. "I didn't mean to."

I frown at her words. I didn't specifically tell her that my study was off limits, but I believed that was implied. My study and my bedroom, although she had already been there. That left my study as the only place where I could keep a part of myself still secret from the world, and especially from her. Now, I didn't have that either. I feel naked and vulnerable, something I hate more than anything else.

"Didn't your parents teach you not to snoop in someone's home?" I snarl at her, only then realizing that my question was totally inappropriate.

Her parents died. She was thrown from foster home to foster home. I know this. I've done a deep background check on her. I should know better than to throw someone's past in their face, especially when it's something they had absolutely no control over. I can immediately tell that she was offended by my comment.

"Actually, they didn't," she snarls back at me. "They died before they could teach me things I could need in my adult life, so I had to learn them on my own," her voice is trembling as she's speaking. I can see pain through that veil of hurt and offence, but I'm blinded by my own rage at her invasion of my privacy.

"It's common sense," I tell her. "You shouldn't go into someone's private rooms. On top of that, you shouldn't break things either."

"I'll clean it up," she adds apologetically.

"No," I snarl, my brows knitting in displeasure. "You've done enough. Just... go."

Her lower lip trembles a little, but she doesn't look away, just to show me that she will do as I request, with that little bit of dignity left and intact. I can see she is barefoot. I could easily go over there, scoop her up and make sure that she doesn't hurt herself on the broken glass. But I don't do that.

She finally looks down, and slowly walks around the shards. As she's walking towards me, I expect to see bloody footprints, but she managed to evade them successfully. There is even a glimmer of victory in the way she is staring me down. Then, she stops right in front of me in the doorway.

"Can you move?" she asks in a demanding tone.

I don't do as she tells me. A part of me wants to grab her by the shoulders, press her against the wall and take her again, until she learns her lesson not to argue with me. But something is preventing me from doing that. I feel like that would mean I surrendered to her, instead of it being the other way around.

I take a step back, allowing her to pass. She does that slowly, and a moment later, I hear the sound of her slamming the door to her room. I remain there for a few moments longer, not really sure what to do. Nothing seems the right course of action.

I try to remind myself that it's just a stupid frame. She didn't break anything of value. But there is more to this. She was in my study, uninvited. She wanted to find out more about me. She could have asked. She should have asked, not go behind my back, snooping around my study.

The thought makes me mad, but somewhere deep down, I can understand. Only... I don't want to understand. This meant that she was doing something I wasn't expecting her to do, which means that I might not have total control over the situation, as I'm used to.

I look down at the glass and decide that I won't be cleaning that up now. I go back to the office and lock myself up for the rest of the afternoon, canceling all my appointments. My secretary seems shocked, but she knows better than to ask. I consider going back home for dinner, but I am still torn between what to do. I don't want to acquiesce. I don't want her to think that she won, that I'm just going to let this one go.

I'm wondering... is it the fact that she's seen Xeena? Now I will have to explain why I'm still keeping a framed photo of another woman in my study. I never had to explain that to anyone. No woman has ever spent the night here. I always took them to my other apartment, which I have just for that purpose.

Irina is the first woman, since Xeena, who was invited into my home. As if that alone wasn't enough, Irina had to go and dig for more where I didn't want her to.

Suddenly, a thought pops to mind. She was just doing what I already did. She had no means of doing a full background check on me, so she did the next best thing. I have to admit that I might have done the same thing if I were her. Hell, I probably would have done that very same thing.

But I can't swallow my pride.

After work, I head to the club. On the way there, I pick up my phone and call Plyn, who answers immediately.

"Everything alright at the apartment?" I ask.

"No suspicious business," he assures me.

"Did the security guys come to take a look?"

"Yes, they just left an hour ago," he replies. "Apparently, the code was input, but the software was disconnected from the main frame for ten seconds, during which someone managed to unlock the door."

"What the fuck?" I growl. "How is that possible?"

"They said they didn't know," I hear him say. "They've never had anything like that happen before."

"Fucking hell," I can't calm down, knowing that this might happen again. "I want you to bring in more people. I want the apartment guarded 24/7. If someone as much as farts in the elevator and the smell climbs up to my floor, I want to know about it. Am I clear?"

"Crystal," he assures me.

"Alright," I nod. "I'm heading to the club for a nightcap. I'll return in about an hour."

"Sure thing, boss," he says, after which I hang up the phone, not feeling as relieved as I thought I would be.

I pocket my phone, looking out of the car window. The line in front of the club is huge, as always. The bouncers are doing a good job separating the rotten apples from the bunch. I have no worries about that. But I never enter through the main door. There is always someone who wants to greet you, meet you. I'm usually not in the mood for that, and I'm especially not in the mood for that now.

I park the car a bit down the street and get out, heading for the small back alley I usually go through when going to the back entrance. There are never any people there, only trash cans and alley cats. Tonight is no different.

I stop somewhere in the middle, reaching into my pocket for my cigarettes. I promised myself I'll quit, but that has to be a perfect moment. Otherwise, I can't do it. This is the least perfect moment, so fuck it.

I take out one and position it loosely between my lips. I flick my lighter on, and the moment I take my first puff, someone punches me on the back of the neck. I immediately drop to the ground, spitting my cigarette out, propping myself up with my hands. I try to inhale deeply, but the moment I do that, sharp pain sears through my entire body, threatening to split it in two.

That is when a second blow comes straight at me. Someone's foot lunges right into the side of my belly and I roll down onto the ground, flat like a pancake. I lift my gaze, but I can't see anything from the pain. The street lamps are hitting the person in the back, leaving his entire silhouette dark, unrecognizable. Whoever this is, is wearing a hoodie which is covering not only his head but also most of his face.

I see he's getting ready to kick me again, so I manage to gather all my leftover strength, grabbing him by the foot before it lands on my stomach. I twist his foot so hard that I hear it crack.

"Aargh!" I hear the silhouette scream in agony.

"Motherfucker..." I get up, spitting blood. The pain is still excruciating, but I know that if I remain lying on the ground, I'm a dead man.

I am leaning to one side, but I'm slowly regaining balance, while the other guy has a twisted ankle. Maybe it's even broken. I can't tell. But from the way he's unwilling to put any weight on it, I can tell it fucking hurts.

He comes at me again, relentless, and I see that I will have to hurt him seriously. This seems like a perfect end to a perfect day, to be honest. Whoever he is, he picked the wrong day to mess with me. I am so filled with rage that I could explode.

I grab him by the neck, lowering him to my side. He tries to punch me again, but I twist his hand, making him drop down to his knees, lifting his elbow high up into the air. I know if I lift any more, his shoulder will break beyond any possibility of repair. I know it, and it seems that he knows it as well.

"Who sent you?" I growl right into his ear.

"Fuck... you..." he spits out, saliva dripping down the corner of his mouth.

I sigh. "I just love it when you guys play hard to get."

I lift his elbow higher up in the air, and the guy screams.

"If I do this again, you know your shoulder will snap," I remind him. "You'll be useless to whoever sent you after me. Now, if you give me a name, I'll let you live. I might even let you go relatively unharmed."

This comment surprises even me. I wasn't expecting such generosity of myself, at a moment when I'm boiling on the inside. But if I said it, I won't go back on my word. Everyone knows this.

"I... can't..." he spits through clenched teeth. "He'll kill me..."

"And you think I won't?" I snarl, close to his ear.

Then, my lack of focus almost costs me my life. The guy picks up a nearby rock and slams it against my temple. An incredible amount of pain clouds my vision, and for a moment, everything gets dark. I hear someone's voice in the distance, then the sound of running footsteps.

"Boss?" I hear Mortar call out to me. "Boss, open your eyes..."

I manage to do that barely, feeling a copper tang in my mouth. I can barely blink. My right eye feels like someone pressed a lit up cigarette on it, and is keeping it there for sheer fun. I reach there with my fingers. It's all wet. Bloody, I presume.

"We'll get him, boss," I hear him say. "Let's get you inside."

"No," I shake my head. "Get me home."

Mortar doesn't say anything to that. He just nods, and I can barely see any of them. He helps me up, then takes me to the car. A few moments later, I feel the gentle rocking of the road underneath the car tires as Mortar drives me back home.

I lean back, wondering what the hell happened. How could I have been so careless? So reckless? I didn't see that the fucker grabbed a rock. He could have killed me, whoever it was. That was probably what he was sent to do, and he almost managed to attain his objective.

Strangely, I'm not enraged. I've gotten used to these attempts on my life, but no one has gotten this close to actually doing it. That is what's got me worried.

I close my eyes, knowing that I am safe... at least for the time being. But a troublesome thought appears in my mind. How can I keep Irina safe, if I can't do the same for myself?

Chapter Thirteen

Irina

I hear the door open, and I immediately jump. I should have apologized immediately, but that stubbornness always gets the best of me. I was wrong and so, I need to apologize. Spending the whole afternoon dwelling on nothing else but that proved it to me, although I have to admit, I knew it before. I just saw how angry he had gotten, and I didn't want to be the one to back down.

I rush to the door, and the moment it opens, I see Mortar holding Hannibal. There is crusted blood in the corner of his mouth. His clothes are torn and dirty. He's holding himself by the sides.

"Oh my God! What happened?" I cry, rushing to the other side to help him walk.

He doesn't say anything at first, just allows Mortar and me to take him to the living room, where he slumps down onto the sofa. I can see immediately that he's in pain. But I don't know if he even wants me here.

"Do you want me to stay?" Mortar ends up asking the same question that is on my mind as well.

I want to tell him that there is no need for him to be here. I can take care of Hannibal on my own. But it's not my place to say any such thing. So, I wait for Hannibal to decide whether he wants us to stay alone together or if he would rather not see me still.

"I'll be fine," Hannibal surprises me with his reply. "Just make sure Plyn stays on guard in front of the apartment. I doubt I can take another assault tonight."

"Sure thing, boss," Mortar nods in that deep voice of his, and instantly, leaves the apartment. The noise from the security system beeps and it means only one thing. Hannibal and I are alone.

I hesitate to look at him in the eye, but the moment I do, I realize he's been staring at me all along.

"Where do you keep the first aid kit?" I ask him.

"In the main bathroom," he tells me, without taking his eyes off me.

And from the way he's talking, I can't tell if he's still mad or not. I just nod, getting up to go, when he grabs me by the elbow. He does it gently, but still firmly enough to let me know that there is something I need to hear.

"You don't have to do this," I hear him say.

"I'd like to think that you would do the same for me, if the roles were reversed," I offer my response, to which I expect him to smile at least, but he doesn't. Instead, he simply lets go of me and I go to the main bathroom, to find what I'm looking for. A minute later, I am back in the living room. He hasn't moved. He is still in the same position that he was when I left him. I sit down next to him, unzipping the bag and trying to find some gauze and saline solution. I locate it quickly, pouring a little bit of the solution on the gauze, then lifting it towards his face.

"I'm just going to clean the wound a little," I say, hoping that he'll understand it as me asking to invade his personal space, something I'm not sure he wants me to do, under the circumstances of us having argued a few hours ago. We still haven't clarified any of that, but attacks take precedence over verbal arguments.

As gently as I can, I proceed to dab the gash on his temple. At first, I thought it would need stitches. It looked horrible, all bloody. But now, with it being a little cleaner, I realize it might not be as bad as I thought it was.

"What happened?" I ask again, still dabbing that same spot carefully.

I'm sure that it's no walk in the park, but he doesn't show in any way that it's painful or even slightly unpleasant. His eyes are open, watching me intently. I try to focus on what I'm doing, without my hand shivering in the process, but it's hard under such a scrutinous gaze.

"I was attacked," he says simply, as if he's talking about the weather, and how I should probably take an umbrella if I'm going out, because it might rain.

"Well, duh," I say without thinking.

This makes him smile. I can see it with the corner of my eyes, as I'm still focused on the gash on his head.

"Who attacked you?" I ask again.

He shrugs instead of a reply. "I don't know, but I'll find out."

I suddenly stop. This time, I look at him straight in the eyes. This is a question I can't look away from.

"Do you think you were attacked because of me?" I hesitate. I'm not even sure I want to know the answer. But I wouldn't be able to keep this question to myself.

His dark brows furrow. I see him wet his lips slightly with his tongue. His beard is hiding this motion only partly. For a moment, I remember how his beard tickled me when he kissed me the first time. And the second time.

I try to banish the thought about kissing. This is neither the time nor the place to be thinking about it.

"No," he shakes his head in reply. I look down at his chest. His shirt is torn open. There is dirt, red scratches. His palms are also bloody. From the looks of it, whoever attacked him, managed to throw him down to the ground. I can't imagine that happening, unless some coward attacked Hannibal from behind, when he wasn't expecting it.

"I am the king of all you see," he tells me, a little more theatrically than I like, but somehow, it suits him. Especially in this vulnerable position, where he yearns to reestablish his dominance again. "There are so many of those who want to steal it away from me. The easiest way would be to just kill me. But, as you can see, I am much tougher to kill than I seem."

"But they did throw you to the ground," I grin, teasing him.

I immediately bite my tongue. I meant it as a joke, but maybe he won't see it as such. Maybe he'll see it as an insult, and that will make our already rocky relationship, or whatever this is that we have, even rockier. I am patiently waiting for his response, when he finally offers it to me.

He tilts his head a little as he speaks, his lips parted enough for me to see his teeth, although his canines are still hidden.

"How do you know that?" he wonders.

I put down the gauze and take his palm with both of my hands. I could have replied easily without touching him, but I couldn't resist the temptation.

"Your palms are dirty," I show him with my fingers, grazing against his dusty, torn skin. "That is proof that you fell down on the ground, but you tried to prop yourself with your palms."

He grins this time. "Very good. I always forget who I'm dealing with here."

"It's best you don't forget that," I smile back, taking the gauze in my hand and proceeding to dab his wound.

"There," I say. "It looks much nicer now. I don't think you even need any stitches."

"You think?" he wonders.

"I've seen worse wounds than that," I nod, pulling away from him, as if I've just realized that we've been too close all this time. "You'll live."

"What would you have done if I hadn't survived?" he suddenly asks me.

I find it incredibly difficult not to burst out into a loud chuckle.

"Is that a trick question?" I ask, putting the saline solution back in the box.

"No," he shakes his head. "It's a normal question."

I think about it for a moment. Should I tell the truth here? He'll probably know if I don't. And the worst part is, I have no idea what I would do.

"I would probably just leave this place," I shrug.

"What about your money?" he reminds me.

"What about it?"

"Wouldn't you think that you earned it?" he continues in this direction.

"Are you asking me if I would steal anything from your home?" I frown, not liking the direction where this is going.

"No, absolutely not," he assures me. "If I thought you were a thief, I wouldn't have left you in here all alone."

"Well..." I shrug again, not really sure what else to do or say. This conversation is proving to be a little deeper than I wanted it to be. And I don't like to open myself up with strangers.

Despite everything, Hannibal is a stranger to me. I slept with him, yes. But just because someone sees your naked body, it doesn't mean that they get to see your naked soul as well. That is far more private, far more intimate.

"Well, what?" he urges. Obviously, he wants to continue this conversation, despite my efforts to redirect it.

"I didn't prove myself worthy of trust, that's for sure," I finally say the words that have been lying heavily upon my heart. Maybe this is the perfect moment for an apology. "I invaded your privacy... and... I'm sorry. I shouldn't have done that."

He grins more widely than I've ever seen him before. He leans back, frowning, but it's more in shock than in displeasure.

"Did you just apologize?" he asks, all incredulous.

"Well, if you're going to make it into such a big deal, I'll take it back immediately," I pout playfully, liking the direction where this is headed much more than remaining in the previous conversation.

"No, don't take it back," he chuckles this time. "I don't kick my opponents while they are down, especially not when they are apologizing."

"So, that is what I am to you, an opponent?" I ask, and this question immediately catches him off guard. I love doing that. He always thinks that he has everything under control. It feels nice to show him that this isn't always possible.

"You know what I meant," he tells me, still smiling. "Also..." he adds, scratching the back of his neck a little nervously. "For what it's worth, I shouldn't have reacted so... rashly."

"Is this your apology?" I ask. I don't want to push him too much, because this apology is already much more than I expected of him. But at the same time, I don't want him to feel self-conscious.

"Yes," he says simply. "That photo... was there for a long time. Much longer than it should have been."

"I'm really sorry that I broke it," I repeat my apology. "I can take it tomorrow to get the glass fixed or get you a new frame. Whatever you want."

"No, none of that," he shakes his head at me determinedly. "This is a sign that the frame doesn't belong there anymore. Or, in my life, for that matter."

I want to ask so many questions about the woman. Most of all, who was she? That question would encompass everything, but I dare not ask. I feel like it's not my place. Still, curiosity gets the best of me, and I am unable to control it.

"Is the woman... still in your life?" This is the safest way in which I can phrase my interest.

It would allow him to answer with a simple yes or no. If he wants, he can elaborate, but if not, then the yes or no would suffice and cut the conversation at the root. Strangely, I feel little beads of sweat on my forehead, as if I asked something monumental. Maybe, I did. Only, I'm not acknowledging the importance of it.

"No," he replies. I wait eagerly to see if he will continue. He hesitates. He looks somewhere behind me, through me, as if he doesn't even see me anymore. "She isn't," he adds. "She belongs to my past. I guess I just don't know how to deal with some aspects of it, and I allowed them to penetrate my present as well. I actually even stopped paying attention to it. I felt like that photo had blended into the interior of my study."

That wasn't a good thing. I could tell that much. If she was present so much as to become a stock part of his surroundings, she must have meant more to him than he wanted to admit.

"But she is out of my life now, and she has been for a long time," he concludes in a way which makes everything crystal clear, even without more explanations.

She was a lover. Of course, she was. They were together, and whatever happened, ended in his heartbreak. That much was obvious. Now, he was telling me that she is no longer in his life. That could be the truth. That could also be himself lying to himself. Which version is true... only time will tell.

Chapter Fourteen

Hannibal

The following morning, I'm the first one to wake up. That is usually the case. I have yet to meet a person who wakes up earlier than me. I make a quick cup of coffee, then some pancakes. It's the least I can do for the way Irina treated me last night, after I've been such an asshole.

My whole body still hurts, but I try to take it easy. I move slowly as I stir all the ingredients, then move onto the frying. It takes me longer than usual, but I'm finally done, arranging the table nicely for the two of us.

I sit down, sipping my coffee and reading the morning news on my phone. Just when I'm about to find out what's going on at the stock market, I hear Irina's door open. Her footsteps follow immediately after, and she appears in the kitchen, those long gazelle-like legs bare and that oversized t-shirt hiding only the uppermost part of her thighs and her succulent butt. It takes all my conscious effort to look at her in the eyes and not her bare legs, or her perked up nipples, about to pierce right through the fabric of her t-shirt.

"Breakfast?" she asks, looking around.

"Just a little something," I shrug.

Her eyes wander around the table, then they meet mine. She looks somehow shocked, incredulous that this happened.

"You don't believe I can cook, huh?" I ask, chuckling. "Although making pancakes can hardly be considered cooking."

"Honestly?" she replies. "I wasn't expecting any of this from you."

"Any of what?" I'm curious now.

"This," she gestures all around her, at the table, at us, at the whole apartment, not really clarifying exactly what she has in mind. "None of this seems like you."

"It just goes to show you," I smile. "Never judge a book by its cover."

"Really?" she laughs aloud this time, and the sound is absolutely heavenly. I don't think I've ever heard her laugh like this, without any constraint. "You're gonna hit me with that old cliché?"

"Clichés are clichés because they make more sense than anything else," I shrug, also chuckling. "Now, come, sit down and have breakfast with me."

She immediately does as she is told, not because it is an order, but because she knows exactly what I meant by it. I feel like the more time we spend together, the less I have to explain myself.

"How are you feeling?" she asks me. "Pain?"

"Bearable," I comment.

"Your gash looks good," she tells me, leaning a bit over the table to take a closer look at the cut on my forehead.

"Good?" I tease her for her word choice.

She pretends to be pouting. "You know what I mean. It doesn't look infected."

"Ah," I nod. "And here I was, thinking I look cool with it. Especially if it leaves a scar."

"Do you want a scar to ruin that pretty face of yours?" she asks, also teasing.

"Now I don't know what part of that to focus on," I pretend to be lost in deep thought. "Should I focus on you thinking that I have a pretty face or the fact that you also think that a scar ruins a pretty face."

"Neither of those two is true," she chuckles. "You're imagining things."

"I must be," I chuckle as well, when suddenly the doorbell interrupts us.

Laughter immediately dies down and we both exchange a worried gaze, although I quickly nod reassuringly.

"It's nothing to worry about," I tell her. "It's probably Plyn or Mortar, with some news regarding the attack."

I walk out of the kitchen, to the front door. I check the keyhole. I was right. I see Plyn standing there with Everild. I welcome them both in, but Plyn excuses himself with work at the club, so only Everild remains behind. I invite him to the kitchen, where he and Irina exchange greetings.

"Why don't I give you two some privacy?" she suddenly gets up from the table, taking her plate of pancakes with her.

"You don't have to do that," I shake my head. While it's true that I don't know if Everild has come for a specific reason or not, I still don't think that there are many things I need to keep hidden from her. She is living with me. If nothing else, that allows her a perspective into my life that no one else has.

"I know," she replies. "But I don't want to listen to you two yap on and on about business stuff. I'll just go read my book in my room," she smiles, as she disappears from the kitchen, and both Everild and I watch her leave, mesmerized.

I've never been the jealous type, and Everild's obvious infatuation with her doesn't go unnoticed. But I know that he would never act on it. At least, not while there is something going on between the two of us.

The truth is that something is going on, only I'm not really sure what. We fucked. OK. That is undeniable. It happened sooner than I thought it would, but it still came as a surprise, especially with her being the initiator.

As soon as Everild and I are left alone, he turns to me. "Heard you got attacked last night. You OK?"

"Word travels fast, huh?" I sigh. I don't know why I thought I could keep it a secret for longer than a few hours.

"I was at the club," he explains. "I went out just when Mortar returned. He told me all about it." I nod. "Do you have any idea who it could be?"

"No," I shake my head. "This is a conversation we already had, you know."

"I know," he confirms. "Do you think whoever attacked you is the same person who tried to break in here?"

"Odds are it is," I reply. "I just have to find out who sent him."

"Who sent him?" Everild wonders curiously. "You think there is someone behind the attack."

"I'm sure of it," I nod. "There's more to this than just a simple attack."

"No attack is simple," Everild reminds me. "Whoever they are, they obviously want you dead."

"Well, they're gonna have to do a lot better than this," I reply.

"That looks nasty," Everild points at the cut on my temple.

"It looks worse than it is," I assure him.

I don't want to admit that I wasn't able to react as usual. The guy caught me off guard. He jumped me from behind, but that's no excuse. I should have been ready. I should have been able to reciprocate adequately, and not like an untrained pup who had no idea what happened.

"I'll ask around," Everild tells me. "See what my guys have heard, if anything."

"Thanks, any help is appreciated."

Everild nods at the door. "How are things with her?"

He doesn't say her name for some reason, although he knows it.

"They're OK," I say.

"Just OK?" he wonders. He always knows when there's something I'm keeping to myself.

"Well..." I shrug. "It could be better, I guess. She found Xeena's photo in my study. I didn't react very well to that."

"Yikes," he says, grimacing awkwardly. "I told you to put it away."

"I know."

"I told you a million times," he adds.

"I know," I repeat. "I should have done it ages ago, but I couldn't."

"Is it because you still love her?" he asks the question that I've been asking myself for a long time now, always with the same, uncertain answer.

When I silently asked myself that last night, while Irina was tending to my wound, I finally knew the real answer. In a way, I didn't know it. I felt it. I felt the lack of all that love that once consumed my entire being. It was gone. Completely gone from my mind, my heart, my body. I have been haunted all these years by the memory of a woman who never treated me well, who only pretended to love me, while I was stupid enough not to see it.

"No," I shake my head. "I don't love her. I think I stopped loving her a long time ago, but it was the memory of what we had that I was still holding onto, that hate, that bitterness."

"I remember how you were when she left you," he speaks carefully.

"I tried hard to forget that, instead of accepting it and then letting go," I explain. "I tried to pretend that it never happened, that she was merely confused and that she would realize her mistake. But the only mistake was that I was blind and stupid."

"Don't be so hard on yourself," Everild tells me. "We all made mistakes in our lives. The most important thing is to learn from them what we can, then let go."

"Exactly," I nod. "I've been lingering in limbo for far too long. Now that Irina is here, I realized that her presence is slowly pulling me out of my shell."

"Are you telling me that you actually think you might have a proper relationship with her?" Everild sounds incredulous.

"I don't think so," I reply. The truth is, I don't know. But I don't want to admit it to anyone, not even myself. I want to keep going along the path that I have chosen, and with the deal that Irina and I have agreed upon. Considering anything more would be a mistake. It might ruin the little that we have, the little that we have managed to create between us.

"No?" he asks again, as if he can sense that I'm not telling him the whole truth.

"No," I say as directly as I can, immediately changing the topic. "What about you? How's your love life?"

He waves his hand dismissively. "You know I don't plan on settling down any time soon."

"You know that we won't be young forever," I chuckle.

"That depends on what you consider young," he laughs along with me.

It feels good to relax with the people you trust. I've learned over the course of time that there are so few people who truly remain loyal in your life, and I've always considered Everild one of them. Just talking to him makes me forget all about the fact that someone is out to get me, and not only me, but Irina as well.

"Have you heard anything about Reyes?" I wonder.

He shrugs. "He's not happy about Irina pulling out of their deal."

"That was to be expected," I confirm.

"But I've heard that he found someone else," Everild tells me in confidence, although he knows that my home is a safe place for anything he might want to divulge.

"Another bounty hunter?" I ask.

"Yes," he nods. "But I don't know who."

"I see," I say, trying to remember who might jump in Irina's place, but no one comes to mind. "That's good. He might forget all about Irina, if he gets what he paid for from someone else."

"It's possible," Everild tells me, but he doesn't sound very convinced. "Reyes is a vengeful bastard."

"That he is," I agree.

"So, you'd best keep her safe," he advises.

I nod. "That is what I'm trying to do."

"Don't go on your own anywhere," he adds. "It's obviously not safe either for you or for her. Always have either Plyn or Mortar with you. That's, at least, my two cents."

"You know your two cents are worth two million here," I smile. "Now, why don't you try some of these pancakes?"

"You made them?" he frowns, chuckling at the same time.

"Yes," I laugh. "Don't be a bastard."

"Fine, fine," he finally gives in, taking my plate and putting a pancake on it, then proceeding to pour maple syrup over it.

Our conversation takes a much lighter turn, and he ends up spending the whole morning there, with Irina joining us back in the kitchen at some point. We were laughing, having fun, talking about the good old days, with Irina listening and laughing together with us. I couldn't remember the last time I felt this relieved, this joyful just because of someone's presence in my life.

I don't know whether to fear this feeling or to welcome it, to be honest.

Chapter Fifteen

Irina

I look at myself in the mirror. With my hair tied all the way into a sleek ponytail and with big, eyesight glasses, I don't look like myself at all. I used make up to define my cheekbones a bit differently as well, and the result is astounding. I'll add a baseball hat to this, and hopefully, that'll provide me with an incognito status while I do some snooping about Hannibal's attack.

I can't do this from inside his home, and I know he won't agree to me going anywhere on my own. But I can't very well have Plyn as my bodyguard and expect people to talk, while he's standing there, looking at them as if he might pound on them at any moment. That's just ridiculous. I need to do this on my own terms.

I take one last look at myself, nodding. Then, I head towards the door. I go down and, of course, there's Plyn sitting in the foyer of the building. He is with his back turned to me, watching the door. I wonder how many people can actually come inside, when the security system feels bullet proof.

Then I remember what happened a few nights ago, and I remind myself that security systems are not all they're cracked up to be. Nothing is bullet proof. Technology has advanced so much today, but no technology can be a match for the human brain. There is always a way around something.

I pat Plyn on the shoulder, but he doesn't flinch, almost as if he expected me to come down at exactly this moment and talk to him.

"Hey," I smile casually.

He turns around and gets up. "Hi," he says, with that questioning look on his face. I try to figure out how old he is. Those eyes look ancient, but I can't see any wrinkles on his face. He looks like he might be in his late twenties. I notice a scar peeking from the collar of his shirt. It looks aged, probably belonging to some old fight or argument that is now mostly forgotten.

"Can you come upstairs for a moment, please?" I ask.

"What's wrong?" he replies with another question. His brows are bushy, placed close together so that it looks like he's constantly frowning. But there is some symmetry to his face, which is making him physically appealing. Attractive, even.

"The light in the kitchen doesn't work," I tell him the first thing that pops to mind.

"The light?" he repeats.

"Yes," I nod. "I don't know what's wrong. Maybe the lightbulb? I mean, I can change it, but I don't know where they are."

"OK," he nods, taking the bait, and heading for the elevator.

I press the button, both of us facing away from each other.

"Aren't you bored just sitting there, doing nothing?" I ask, hoping to make small talk, to get him distracted. But he doesn't seem chatty at all.

"I'm doing my job," he corrects me, without turning to face me, but rather keeps staring in front of him, waiting for the ping of the elevator.

"Of course, you are," I nod, sighing silently. I just hope the elevator arrives quickly.

Fortunately, it does. The door opens, Plyn steps inside first. Just as I'm about to enter, I pat myself on the forehead.

"How silly of me," I smile as I speak. "I was supposed to check the mail. Hannibal asked me to."

Plyn is still looking at me, as if he doesn't understand. I gesture at him with my hand, taking a step back.

"Why don't you head on upstairs, while I go back to the mailbox?" I suggest, but he doesn't look convinced. "I won't be leaving the building, I promise."

That is, of course, a lie. But he doesn't know that... yet.

Not waiting for him to reply, I press the button to close the doors and I take another step back. Before he can say anything, I'm out of sight, with a sigh of relief. I rush to the door, knowing that I don't have much time before he notices I'm gone. I know he won't be happy about that. Neither will Hannibal. But I have to help him. I have to see if I can find out more about this attack, whether it's really Reyes who's behind it or if there's another enemy playing the game.

That's exactly why I contacted an old friend.

Well, maybe friend isn't the right word. The right word would be a vampire I could have killed, but didn't, and now he's repaying that favor by telling me what he's heard on the street about some people or vampires I know. It's a good deal, to be honest.

I hail the first cab I find, and I head to our usual meeting spot. It's a rarely frequented biker bar, on the outskirts of the city, where no one in their right mind would come, unless they're crazy bikers. Quinn is crazy, but he can't pass for a biker. Still, he knows a few guys here who buy him drinks, so he kinda blends in when he's inside.

I push the saloon-like doors open and enter from broad daylight into what appears to be Dracula's lair. The lights are barely there, and I feel like I'm about to reach out and start feeling for things around me at any moment. The bartender is a lady who seems to be over fifty but refuses to accept that, with red lips and a black eyeliner. She's wiping a beer glass, and gives me just a passing glance, despite the fact that I stick out like a sore thumb.

Finally, I see Quinn in the corner booth, trying to hide behind a beer glass. I immediately head over there.

"Hey," I greet him as soon as I sit down.

He frowns instead of a reply. "How many more times?" he snorts.

"As many as I say," I remind him. "You want another beer?"

"Is that gonna cost me more meetings with you?" His voice is snarky, but that's how he always is. He hates the world and everyone in it, but I've got him by the balls. He hates that even more.

"No," I smile. "Listen... you caught me in a good mood. You tell me what you know about the attack on Hannibal Delacruz, and we'll be even for good."

His eyes widen in shock. I've never said this before, and he knows I mean it. Hell, I plan on leaving this lifestyle behind. Hopefully, when I do, I won't need to meet guys like this ever again. So, I might as well use this last chance to squeeze him dry of anything he might know about the attack.

"You promise?" he asks.

"Do you believe it when people give you a promise?" I wonder.

"No," he grimaces.

"Then, why does it matter whether I'll give you my word or not?" I chuckle. Sometimes, Quinn's negativity can be fun. But only in small doses. So can his body odor. "You know, you should really take a shower. You stink." I pull away as I say that, and at that moment, the overly made up bartender slash waitress comes over to us.

"Hey," she grunts in a deep, masculine voice.

"Hey," I reply, trying to sustain my shock at the depth. "Can we get two beers, please?"

"Sure," she says again, then leaves us alone.

I turn my attention back to Quinn. "So, what do you say?"

"I don't know anything," he shrugs.

"Come on," I frown. "You can do better than that. It's your freedom we're talking about here."

He inhales deeply, as if he's carried the heaviest burden on his back. "I don't know anything," he repeats. "But I may be able to find out, if you give me a day or two."

"One day," I tell him, not even sure if I'll be able to leave the apartment again after this. Hannibal will watch me even closer. "That's how much I can give you."

"OK," he nods. "But you're getting me into a shitload of trouble here."

"Why?" I wonder.

He looks around, as if he's half-expecting someone to listen in on our conversation. Everyone seems to be minding their own business. But still, you never know.

"There's talk of a big overturn," he lowers his voice as he's talking, his face getting closer to mine. Even now, I can smell him better than I can see him.

"What kind of an overturn?" I ask as quietly as him.

"They say there's a conspiracy against the king," he adds, with fear in his voice. I've heard the way fear sounds many times. I could never mistake it for anything else. "They want him dead. And they'll stop at nothing."

"But... who is this they?" I demand silently.

He pulls back and shrugs. "I don't know. If I did, do you think I'd be sitting here, telling you? I'd probably be a dead man. A dead vampire, that is."

At that moment, the lady comes, bringing our beers.

"Thanks," I say, and she just nods. I appreciate such lack of conversation on occasions such as this one and make a mental note to leave her a good tip. "You have to give me something."

"What if it gets me killed?" he squeezes through clenched teeth. "What good is it to me then that you'll leave me alone when someone else will slit my throat from ear to ear?"

Suddenly, an idea comes to me. I can ask for some money from Hannibal. I could tell him I've got some debts I need to settle. And I could use that money to help Quinn leave town, go wherever he thinks he'll be safe.

"What if I can get you some money for that info?" I ask, lowering my tone as much as I can.

He looks at me suspiciously, as if I'm offering some food and he's sure it's poisoned, but he's starving.

"How much?"

"How much do you need?"

"Five grand," he tells me. His tone is careful, signaling that he spat out the first number that came to mind. I could probably haggle, make him go lower, but I don't want to do that. I'll be getting more than enough from Hannibal once this whole shitstorm comes to an end.

"Five it is," I nod, much to his shock.

"Where the fuck did you get that kind of money?" He grabs me by the hand. I can feel his clammy touch on my skin. He knows I've always been short on money, so of course he's surprised.

"That's none of your concern," I pull my hand away. "I can get you the money as soon as tomorrow."

I don't know why I'm claiming this, but I want him assured of payment, as much as I want to be assured of getting that info tomorrow. It's a win-win.

"OK," he nods finally. "I'll see what I can find out. You better have that money, Irina, or..."

"Or else?" I tilt my head, giving him a disbelieving look. "Are you seriously planning on threatening me? After everything we've been through?"

I see his Adam's apple bobble down, then back up as he swallows heavily. He wasn't expecting me to say that.

"Just see what you can find out. Don't worry about the money."

I get up, drink half of my beer in one go, then turn around and walk over to the bar. I leave her a twenty. She just nods. I nod back. I love it when people understand each other with just a nod, no words. The world would be such a happier place without all the misunderstandings caused by words.

With those thoughts, I exit the bar and head back to Hannibal's place, ready to be scolded like a teenager who not only snuck out of the house, but also stayed out way past curfew.

Chapter Sixteen

Hannibal

"Where the hell have you been!?" I shout as soon as I open the door, and she just stands there, looking like a soaking wet kitten.

"Can I come inside, and then I'll explain everything?" she asks with a playfully sad pout.

I frown, but I stand aside, letting her in. I close the door behind her, like an enraged parent. She walks over to the living room, probably listening to the sound of my footsteps behind her, but she doesn't turn around. She sits down on the sofa, expecting a scolding. I can't even sit down. I'm beyond myself with worry.

"I sent Plyn to find you," I tell her, not sure where else to start. There is a mixture of sensations inside of me, anger and relief, but mostly its leaning towards the side of relief, so I can't start off by telling her that she's not leaving this apartment until I tell her she can. Besides, I doubt telling Irina something like that would work. She's not the type that takes orders very well. After all, that is one of the reasons why I chose her. It's not just the fact that she is beautiful and smart, but she is also stubborn, capable, unafraid and unapologetic. However, telling her all of this now would be the worst of all moments.

"He's still out there, looking for you," I frown.

"I do owe him an apology," she chirps, as she pulls up her legs on the sofa, bends them in the knee and sits on her feet.

"Do you mind explaining this whole mess now?" I say, trying to sound as calm as I can, but it's hard. She obviously thinks this is a joke, as if she's never been in this world, as if she doesn't know that people disappear just like that, and she could as well, unless she lets me protect her.

"I wanted to find out who attacked you," she reveals, staring at me dead in the eye, as if that would clear her of all her transgressions.

"And you would die in the process?" I frown.

"No," she shakes her head. "Why would you think that?"

"Are you serious?" my brows knit even more, and I feel a headache coming on. "You've seen what's happened. Someone broke into my apartment. Someone tried to kill me, and they were almost successful at that. You were damn lucky that you went out and nothing happened to you."

"I took precautions," she tells me. "See?"

She takes off her glasses and pulls the hair tie off of her hair, so that now it's framing her face as usual, falling down her shoulders on both sides. I can tell that her face also looks slightly different, as if she's done something to it with make up.

"No one recognized me," she assures me.

"You were lucky," I repeat.

"I took precautions," she echoes, with a smile.

I inhale deeply, realizing that there is no arguing with her. I grab my phone and send Plyn a quick message, urging him to come back, that Irina is here. Then, I put it back in my pocket.

"Did you clean your wound today?" she suddenly asks.

"No," I tell her. "I've already forgotten all about it."

"You can't do that," she says, jumping from the sofa, rushing to the main bathroom, and returning with the saline solution and some gauze. She sits back down, turned to me. "It looks fine, but let's clean it, just to be on the safe side."

I don't say anything to that. I know what she's trying to do. She's trying to shift focus away from what she's done, so we'd stop talking about it.

I guess I can understand her point of view to some extent. She's not used to being limited in this way. She is advised to stay inside, otherwise something might happen to her. That's not a reality anyone would be able to accept with ease, especially someone with a mind of their own, like hers.

She proceeds to pour a little bit of the saline solution onto the gauze, then dabs it gently against my temple. This time, it only feels cold and slightly unpleasant. There is no stinging sensation. Only a sense of concern on her part.

"You could have been a nurse, you know," I tell her, staring straight ahead of me, while her eyes are focused on what she's doing. Her delicate fingers are moving with ease and grace.

"Really?" she chuckles, not looking at me. "That never occurred to me."

"It seems like something that would suit you better, saving someone rather than killing them," I point out.

She twitches barely perceptibly, but I noticed. I don't think she liked my comment, the way I addressed her responsibility at killing those she had to kill.

"I didn't mean it as an offense," I add. "We all do what we need to do to survive."

She swallows heavily, her lips parting as she's so close to me that she is almost touching my cheek with them.

"When I was a kid, I didn't think I would grow up to be a vampire killer, if that's what you mean," she says sounding a bit off.

"I think most of us don't grow up to do the job our kid selves expected us to," I shrug.

She pulls away to finally look at me, and I don't like the way she does it. "You grew up to be a king, a billionaire. I doubt your past kid self is displeased." But a moment after she says it, she smiles. "You did good, Hannibal Delacruz. You should be proud."

"Aren't you proud of yourself?" I ask. She dabs my temple a few more times, and then puts the gauze down onto the small coffee table in front of us.

"Not really," she admits with a defeated tone of voice.

I hate hearing her like this. I want to grab her by the shoulders and remind her of all the wonderful things that she does, that she is, because she seems to have forgotten all about them. I want to kiss her breathless, take her to the bedroom and make love to her for the rest of the day, until we can't sit up straight any longer, but only lie on the bed, exhausted in each other's arms.

Yet, I don't do any of that. It seems like a transgression on my part this time. This is, after all, still just a deal the two of us have, although I realize that I am slowly falling for her.

Falling for someone is a dangerous path, one I've traveled already, one I don't want to set another foot on again.

"I'm not satisfied with myself or my life at all," she continues without being asked to, and I realize that she is dying to get this off of her chest. So, I let her. I am listening to her without a word, just looking at her, nodding occasionally, allowing her to say whatever it is that is bearing heavily upon her soul.

I know what it is like to carry a burden which you feel you can't share with anyone. Being on the top is something everyone wishes for, but at the same time, it is lonely on the top. There aren't many people there. There aren't many friends there you can share your joys and sorrows with. There are mostly just people who would gladly stab you in the back, as I've had happen so many times before.

Even now, I know that my life is on the line. I know that it is hanging by a thread, and I have no idea who it is that is threatening it. It could truly be anyone in my surroundings.

"That is why I will disappear when you and I finish this deal," she concludes, placing her hands in her lap helplessly. "I want to start my life somewhere new, somewhere where I can look at the sunset every single evening, maybe a little house by the sea somewhere far, far away. I don't know... all I know is that I don't want to stay here. When I go, I doubt that I will return ever again."

The thought of her never returning, never seeing her again, clenches at my heart, violently creating a gap of pain and sorrow. I never thought that there would be a moment where I might want to see her, and I would not be able to.

But if that is what she has chosen for herself, then that is what she has to do.

"Everyone creates their own path in life," I remind her. "Money isn't everything in the world, but I know that it is still a means for us all to get what we want."

"Exactly," she nods. "I never considered myself a materialistic person. I always thought I'd need just a little bit of money to get by. But that's not true. That's not life in this city. It can eat you up alive, if you are poor, if you let it."

I want to tell her that I would keep her safe no matter what, that I would provide her with whatever she could possibly need, but I don't say any of that. It is just a thought that lingers inside my mind, like a haze, about to disperse and disappear.

Suddenly, I can't control myself any longer. I cup her face with my hands, bringing her close to me. Our lips meet gently, softly. It isn't a passionate kiss that promises a wild night of love making. It is a much different kiss, the result of what she just shared with me, and the way she did it.

She responds immediately. Her body reacts to mine as if they were made for each other, and only now that we have found each other can our bodies truly be themselves.

She slides her tongue into my mouth unexpectedly, but I immediately follow. My hands go down to her breasts, cupping them softly. They are pure perfection, the way they fit into my palms so perfectly. I want to wrap my lips around those perked up nipples, to suck on them while she moans in pleasure.

My cock twinges at the thought, feeling heavy in the constraints of my pants. She lowers her hand to feel it, and it thickens immediately, responding to her touch.

"Let's go to bed," she murmurs against my lips, and just as I'm about to get up, lift her into my arms and follow her command, the doorbell is heard.

We exchange a meaningful glance, and her lips erupt into a smile.

"Well, someone has perfect timing," she points out.

"It's probably Mortar," I say with a sigh. "I'm expecting him to bring me some reports from the club."

"Raincheck for tonight?" she whispers, gently brushing her nose against mine.

"You bet," I agree, kissing her lips one more time, then heading to the door, adjusting my raging, disgruntled cock in my pants.

Chapter Seventeen

Irina

I leave Hannibal and Mortar to discuss business, while I go back to my room. I close the door, remembering how worried and upset Hannibal was. A part of me is surprised. Does he care about me that much? Do I mean something to him? The thoughts make me feel... giddy.

Ugh. There's that word again, making me sound like a fifteen year old in love with someone she's not supposed to be in love with. The truth is, I shouldn't be in love with Hannibal Delacruz. That would be the worst possible thing to happen. This is just a deal we have. He scratches my back, I scratch his.

And his concern about my disappearance today is just him worried that he might not uphold his part of the bargain. Nothing else. The sex is just a cherry on top. I started it. So, of course he thinks it's OK now. And it is OK.

Ugh. I feel so confused. I shake my head at myself as I walk into the bathroom and run hot water into the bathtub. Maybe a nice, long, relaxing bath will soothe me and wash all my troubles away. If only there was a way to truly do this.

I take off my clothes and look at myself in the mirror. I forgot that I put on so much make up. I barely look like myself. I use soap and warm water to wash all the dirt and make up away, and when I lift my face to gaze at the mirror again, I recognize all my facial features. Those are my eyes, my cheeks, my smile.

I press my fingertips to my face, wondering. There are so many thoughts racing inside my mind right now, and they all revolve around Hannibal Delacruz.

I turn around, realizing that there's enough water in the tub, unless I want to flood the whole place. I stop the water, sinking into the bath, allowing the warmth to envelop me completely. I close my eyes, losing myself in the sensation.

I refuse to open my eyes. If I keep them closed, I can convince myself that this isn't just a temporary dream. There is a possibility that I will stay here with him, and we will share a life together, share everything together.

I smile without even realizing what I'm doing. But the truth is, I'm just existing here on borrowed time. We've added sex into the equation, but I know that Hannibal isn't looking to settle down. Otherwise, he would... wouldn't he?

And if he did want to settle, why on earth would the vampire king want to settle with a nobody like me? A bounty hunter even. Those things just don't go together.

I sigh heavily, finally opening my eyes. Maybe life is all about enjoying the moment, I think to myself. I should appreciate what I have here and now and think about what will happen later... later.

Whether or not I might be heartbroken that I'm no longer with him, well... that is something that I will deal with when the time comes. No use in worrying about that now.

As if beckoned by my thoughts, there is a knock on the door and Hannibal peers in.

"Are you decent?" he grins. He obviously sees what I'm doing, and that no, I'm not decent at all. But I do love his boyish charm. This is where I need to stop my heart, in thoughts such as this one, because it is this charm, among other things, that I will miss when I leave this place. When I leave him.

"Not at all," I smile back. "But I see that doesn't stop you."

"Never did," he confirmed, walking into the bathroom, and getting down on his knees by the bathtub.

There are bubbles inside, hiding most of my body from plain sight, which is making it even more erotic. I lift my foot out of the water and rest it on the side of the bathtub. He watches me do it intently.

"Do you want me to wash your back?" he suddenly asks.

"Sure," I say, without thinking.

I lean forward, revealing my back to him. He rolls up his shirt sleeves slowly, sensually. I never thought seeing a man do this could be such a turn on. Then again, everything this man does is a turn on. It's just the way he is, the way he exists, the way he transforms everything into sheer desire.

He uses his palm to remove the leftover foam, then traces his fingers along my skin softly. I giggle when he reaches my armpit.

"I had no idea you were ticklish," he says with a chuckle.

"Just a little," I admit, turning my head to face him, then resting it on my bent knees.

He takes a sponge from a small basket by the bathtub and shoves it into the water. It grazes against my inner thigh, stopping just before my pussy. I suppose that was the intention. I close my eyes, enjoying the sensation. He then presses the sponge against my pussy, removing it quickly and squeezing it dry onto my back. Slowly, he starts to rub my back with it, in gentle, circular motions.

"That feels so good," I murmur.

He keeps on doing it, then I lift my head, and look at him with an impish expression on my face.

"You look a bit dirty," I grin. "Why don't you come in and clean yourself off?"

"I thought you would never ask," he grins back at me, releasing the sponge back into the water, then getting up.

He unbuttons his shirt slowly, one button at a time. It's painfully slow. I want to see all of him. I want to touch and kiss all of him. I want to feel his hands on my body more than ever now.

He allows his shirt to fall down to the floor. He stops to look at me.

"Are you enjoying the show?" he asks roguishly. A small curl fell over his forehead, making him appear even more boyish, as if no matter what he did, you would always forgive him. All he needed to do was look at you with those puppy dog eyes, and you would be his forever.

As I'm looking at him now, that is my greatest fear. Being his forever.

Forever is a long time to belong to someone who doesn't want you. Heck, forever is a long time to belong even to someone who does want you. But I know what he wants from me. He was clear about that from the start. I was also clear about what I needed from him. I don't know why I had to go and make everything more complicated than it needed to be.

"I would pay good money to see this show," I chuckle, pointing at his pants. "Continue."

"As my lady wishes," he flashes me a row of those pearly whites through his beard.

There is something about a man with a beard. Something powerful, demanding, masculine. I always liked guys with a little bit more hair on them, and Hannibal is pure perfection in every way. It's no wonder that all the women, human and vampire, want a piece of him. You would sell your soul for a night with him. And many have. In fact, I'm sure I've done that very same thing myself.

My soul doesn't feel like it belongs to me any longer. It's his. It's all his. My mind, my heart, my body. I know that as much as I know that the sun rises in the east and sets in the west. There is nothing that would change that.

My forever would be a very long time without him, but perhaps I can take some solace in the fact that we did spend some time together, relishing each other's company. He is mine now. Perhaps that is all you can ask of a person. To belong to you in the present moment, without any promises for the future. Then, when that present moment is gone, you just return that person to where it was, to where you found it, because that person doesn't belong to you anymore. It actually never belonged to you in the first place. You were all living on borrowed time.

He undoes his belt. I hear that clinking sound. Then, the button. But the moment he's about to let them drop down to the ground, there is the sound of the doorbell.

We both look in the direction of the door at the same time.

"Are you fucking kidding me!?" he snarls at the door, at whoever is standing there, sounding extremely pissed.

"I don't think it's meant to be today," I chuckle.

He looks at me without any annoyance. There is something in his eyes, something I can't quite decipher. He is a difficult man to read. I guess it comes with the territory.

"Tonight?" he asks.

"Unless we have more unexpected guests," I point out, more than amused that our efforts at having fun were thwarted twice already.

"That should be Plyn," he tells me. "Back from trying to find you."

"That's what you get for trying to find people who aren't lost in the first place," I tease. "You waste time."

"You need to be punished for what you did," he grins, with a flicker of something naughty in his eyes, as he buckles up his belt, then bends down to grab his shirt. He slides his arms inside, then proceeds to button it up. A few moments later, he looks like nothing happened. Or better yet, like nothing was about to happen.

"You have some specific punishment in mind?" I ask playfully, lying back in the bathtub, allowing my breasts to peek from out of the water. My nipples are already hard at the thought of the sex we could have had in the tub.

"You have no idea what I would do to you now," he growls fervently, his eyes devouring my breasts.

"Tonight," I remind him. "You can punish me then as well, but only if it has something to do with your palms and my bare behind."

"Ugh, you tease," he grins at me, lowering his hand to his crotch and adjusting himself a little.

"A problem?" I wink.

"Nothing I won't be able to solve tonight," he says. "I'm going. If I stay a moment longer, I'll have to fuck you right here."

The way he says it so openly sends thrills through my entire body, and I do wish he would make good on that promise, right here, right now. But I know he can't make Plyn wait in front of the door.

"Enjoy your bath," he says as he heads out the door, closing it behind him.

My gaze lingers in that direction for a few seconds longer, half-expecting him to come back and do what he said he would. My pussy throbs at the idea. I consider pleasuring myself in the water, at the thought of him spanking me, licking my pussy, fucking me senseless, but I opt against it. I would rather wait for tonight.

I take the sponge and slowly start rubbing it all over my body. It's not nearly as pleasant as when he did it. I fear nothing will be as pleasant without him. But that's life. You only know that something wonderful happened to you because when it's gone, you miss it terribly.

That is how I will miss Hannibal Delacruz. Terribly. Dreadfully. Completely.

Forever.

Chapter Eighteen

Hannibal

As soon as I close the door to Irina's room, it takes all my conscious effort not to rush back and fuck her into oblivion. The sight of her in that bathtub aroused me more than I ever thought I could be.

Instead, I go to the door, and open it. I see Plyn standing in front. I invite him in.

"Coffee?" I offer.

"Sure," he nods, following me into the kitchen.

I put the coffee on, as he takes a seat.

"So, she's back?" he asks.

"Went to do some digging on her own," I shrug. "Women."

"I would have followed her, but she screwed me over," he explains.

"I know," I smile. "Don't worry. No harm done. But we have to be extra vigilant, so she doesn't do that again. She might not be that lucky."

"I agree," he nods.

"Any news about the attack?" I ask.

"Nothing," he shakes his head. "Word on the street is that Reyes found someone else."

"Ah, that's good," I nod, waiting for the coffee to boil. As soon as it's done, I pour two cups, placing one of them in front of him, then taking a seat opposite Plyn at the kitchen table.

"And of course, there's always some conspiracy going on, about your assassination," he adds, as he takes his first sip.

"I know," I nod. "But this feels different."

"It is different," Plyn assures me. "No one has dared come after you here. That shows balls."

"I agree. It proves that whoever is behind this attack means business. They didn't mean to just frighten me or overthrow me. They mean to kill me. Seriously."

"Maybe it's a good idea to stay at home these days," he suggests, as he eyes me from across the table.

"You know I always value your input," I assure him. "But you know I can't stay home for days. I can't run my business remotely. I need to be there, in person."

"Let me or Mortar handle it," he advises. "Mortar can handle the club, as he's been doing these days."

"I know the club is in good hands with him. What about the company?" I wonder.

"Manage it from here," he shrugs. "Have conference calls when you need to. If there's anything that needs to be brought physically to you for anything, have them bring it over. A few days of you laying low shouldn't make any difference."

What he's suggesting doesn't sound half bad. I could stay here, do whatever needs to be done, and keep a closer eye on Irina. I doubt she'll do another stunt like that again, but you never know with women, especially women like her.

Then, I remember why she said she did it. She wanted to find out who attacked me. The thought fills me with strange sensations, exactly the kind that I've been trying to avoid. But it's difficult not to feel anything, to prevent yourself from feeling, when there is someone like Irina standing right in front of you.

She deserves the best. Before, I didn't know her. Before, I thought this could just be a business transaction. We could both get what we wanted from the other. But now, I'm desperately trying to fight off this emotion, this need to have everything with her.

"Maybe you're right," I say, banishing these thoughts and reverting to the present moment, where I'm sitting in my kitchen with Plyn, and

Irina is still here. There are only a few walls that are separating us. But we might as well be worlds apart, as we are.

"You know I'm right," Plyn grins.

"OK," I nod. "I'll stay home for a few days."

Plyn downs his coffee, then gets up. "I'd better get back to my post."

"Thanks," I tell him, although I'm sure he already knows it.

We've been through thick and thin, and when you're in a position of power, it's crucial to have a small handful of men you would trust your life with. If you don't have that, you won't make it on your own. I've seen too many vampires rely solely on themselves, not wanting to be vulnerable to an attack, but it turned out that you can't rely solely on yourself. It's just one person. It's not enough. You can't be enough to yourself.

I wonder if love functions the same way. Maybe it does. Ever since Xeena broke my heart, I haven't really been thinking much about love. To be honest, I haven't thought about love at all. I decided to cut it out of my life completely, like a tumor, because that's what love is. It lies to you first, that everything will be alright, that you will get your happily ever after, but then it breaks you completely, leaving you for dead. I know that feeling. I know it, and I never want to go through that again.

I walk Plyn out, then consider knocking on Irina's door, just to see what she's doing. But I opt against it. Perhaps we've grown too close these days. Her presence feels good, but I have to keep reminding myself that this is just temporary. If I allow her into my heart, then I am giving her permission to break it. She might promise that she won't, but one can make many promises in the present, then the circumstances might change, and all those promises go out the window. After all, isn't that exactly what happened with Xeena?

With those thoughts plaguing my mind, I pass by Irina's door and head for my study. I close the door on the inside and sit down at my desk. I grab my phone and dial Everild. He picks up immediately.

"Hey," he greets me.

"Hey," I say back. "Did I catch you at a bad time?"

"No, nothing like that," he assures me. "Everything OK?"

"Yeah," I nod, leaning back into my chair. "I just wanted to tell you that I won't be at the office these days."

"Why not?"

"Plyn advised me to take it easy, and I think he's right. I don't like to admit it but being attacked like that reminded me that I'm not the vampire that I used to be. I'm getting old. I need to be more careful, otherwise..." I don't finish the sentence, but we both know what I'm referring to.

"You old?" he echoed on the other end of the line. "No way."

"You're my best friend," I chuckle. "You're supposed to say that."

"So, you're staying home then?"

"Yeah," I confirm. "I'll see what I can do from here. That's why I'm calling to let you know if you want to talk business details, just drop by here whenever you feel like it."

"Are you sure I won't be interrupting anything special?" he asks, with a hint of curiosity in his voice.

I chuckle. "We've been interrupted twice today already."

"Twice?" I hear him laugh. "How many times a day can you do it? And here you are saying you're old. You're a fucking machine."

I'm unable to resist laughing at this. "I'm far from a machine. If I were a machine, I wouldn't have gone down so easily when they attacked me. But thanks for the pep talk."

"Whoever they were, they were some cowards who didn't have the balls to attack you face to face, and instead, had to surprise you, because they knew you'd beat them otherwise."

I smile at his reasoning. A few years back, I would have thought the same thing. I was in the peak of my power. But now... I feel like this is the sunset. Maybe that's for the better. No one is meant to rule forever.

I try to banish those thoughts from my mind. I'm still on the top. I am still the king. If they want to kill me, they'll have to do a helluva lot better than that, because I'll be extra careful now. I still have a few years of rule ahead of me, and I plan on making the best of them.

"Thanks," I tell him.

"For what?" he asks, sounding surprised.

"For everything," I tell him. "For being a friend. I don't have many people who have been with me through everything. You are one of them. Even when your own life wasn't going perfectly, you put all that aside, and you helped me achieve my goals."

"I knew that once I helped you, you would help me," he reminds me.

I always knew that he sacrificed his own aspirations for mine. He never put himself first, although there were times where he should have. I felt like sometimes, I was too selfish, but he always assured me that some vampires were destined for greatness, and some were destined to help that greatness be achieved.

I never considered him anything less than me. Somehow, he decided that on his own. He pushed for my goals to be met. His took a backseat to mine. He never whined. He never moaned. He never said one word that might have indicated his displeasure with this.

He has been following my path in life loyally, and when most of my goals were met, I knew that it was time to focus on what he wanted in life. I helped him obtain the position of the clan leader, which he still occupies. Currently, we are working on some business transactions that will eventually bring him a lot of money. That's his reward for being a loyal, patient friend, the likes of which I know I will never be able to find again.

We exchange a few more pleasantries, then he says that he will stop by the following day, and this is where we end the conversation. I hang up, inhaling deeply, wondering if I could focus on some work. I open my laptop and turn it on. I have numerous unread emails, most of which require my urgent attention.

I start with the first one, then slowly move onto the second, third, fourth. It's difficult to focus, but I manage somehow.

The only thing that is distracting me is the knowledge that Irina is in the same place I am. I could just go over to her, grab her by the waist, pull her close to me and kiss her senseless, tearing all the clothes off her. But that would only make me even more unable to focus.

So, I remain at my desk, focused on emails that don't seem to make any sense, because my mind sees them as blurs, as random numbers and words, and not a meaningful unit.

Chapter Nineteen

Irina

The following day, Hannibal and I have breakfast. I notice that something is off. It's almost as if he is pulling away from me. Maybe he's still a little upset that I went out on my own?

When I asked him that, he assured me that we were fine, as long as I didn't do that again. The truth is, I was hoping to meet Quinn, to see if he has any news regarding the attack. But I doubt that I will be able to go. I managed it once. Twice would be too much.

Perhaps I would be able to convince Plyn to come with me, but I doubt Quinn would be OK talking in front of a stranger. That means I can either find a way of somehow sneaking out of the house alone or just call him on the phone instead.

I'm not a big fan of talking to people on the phone, to be honest. I like to see their facial expressions, not just hear the words they're saying. Because sometimes, the two can differ greatly. Usually, the words they say can be faked, but a facial expression or some tick is always a dead giveaway. This is crucial, especially when you're in the line of work I am.

I sit on the bed in my room, and I take my phone. It's the afternoon already, so hopefully, Quinn has something for me. I dial impatiently, then wait for him to pick up.

"Yes?" he answers.

"Hey, it's me," I say.

"Oh." He doesn't sound too thrilled. I guess I wouldn't be either, if I were him, so I don't hold it against him.

"Do you have something for me?" I ask.

He waits for a moment before replying. "Why are we doing this over the phone? We never do it over the phone."

"I can't meet up with you," I admit.

"Why?" he asks, sounding suspicious. "Is it because you don't have the money?"

Of course, that would be the first thing he would think of. The money. Again, I can't blame him. He needs money even more than I do. There are more people out to get him than vampires I killed. And that's a lot.

"I have the money," I assure him. "It's in my bank account. Two clicks and I can transfer it to yours."

I remember the quick conversation I had with Hannibal. He didn't even question my need to get some of the money upfront. In fact, he asked if I needed more than five grand, to which I replied that would be enough. Two clicks, and the money was transferred to my account. Now, I can do the same to Quinn, only I'm not sure if he even has an account. You never know with such people.

"I'd rather have cold, hard cash," he tells me over the phone. "Non-traceable. Immediately at my disposal. That's what I like about it."

I frown. "Well... can't you just get it from the atm or something? Come on. Don't be a dick."

I hear him sigh on the other end of the line. I know he's thinking about it, considering his options. That's what we're all doing. "This is some big shit, Irina," he suddenly tells me in a tone I've never heard him use.

"What do you mean?" I ask, my eyes widening in anticipation of what I might find out.

"I'd really rather talk about this in person," he reveals.

"Can't you just tell me quickly?" I ask. "This is a safe line, you know this."

"Well... I pulled in a few favors, one from a guy who works in Hannibal's company, in the financial department," he pauses, as if trying to find the right words. Then, he continues in the same note. "He tells me that some money's been disappearing, and not small amounts, either."

"Someone's embezzling money from the company?" I ask.

"Yes," he confirms. "We're talking millions."

"How come no one's noticed it?"

"My guy says it's hidden inside other losses that the company suffered in the last couple of years. So, everyone just assumed that it all went together, but in fact it didn't."

"What does your guy think?" I wonder.

"It has to be someone close to the company, someone who knows what's going on. Maybe even someone who's in constant contact with Hannibal himself."

"That could be any of the employees at the company," I frown.

"No," he corrects me. "It has to be someone on a top level, if it's someone from the company. Someone who can sweep away all the evidence and make it seem like it never happened."

"Aha," I nod, more to myself than to him.

"Also, I asked him to dig as deep as he can, and he said he stumbled onto a company while he was going through the paper trail," he tells me.

"What company?"

"Apparently, it's some small construction company that builds houses in the mountains. That's what they specialize in. At least, that's what my source could tell me."

"What's the name?"

"Wait, it was something very obscure," he tells me. "Asmodeus Co."

I grimace. "Never heard of it."

"Me neither," he agrees. "I tried finding them online. Nothing. No trace of them anywhere."

"How does your inside guy know of it then?" I frown.

"Because he has connections on the dark web, duh." I can hear his sarcasm from the other end of the line. It's reaching me loud and clear.

"Whoever owns this company has made sure to keep its existence a secret."

"Do you have anything concrete, like physical evidence, some documents, anything, to back this up?" I ask.

"I have the whole paper trail," Quinn tells me. "To be honest, I'd gladly dump all this on you, take my money and just be on my merry way, if you don't mind."

"I don't mind. You'll just have to come see me. I can't go anywhere."

"You've already said that," he points out. "What, are you being kept a prisoner?"

I almost chuckle out loud. "Sort of."

"Sort of?" he repeats. "Seriously, Irina... are you in trouble? Do you need help?"

This reaction reminds me that although we have a mostly hate relationship, because I almost killed him, let's face it, sometimes there is also some love peppered in there. He does care about me, or perhaps he just cares about his five grand. In any case, I appreciate the offer to help.

"I'm fine," I assure him. "I'm at Hannibal's place."

"Wait... Hannibal Delacruz?" I can hear the shock, the suspicion, the utter disbelief in his voice. To be quite honest, I also wouldn't believe it if some bounty hunter told me that he or she is staying with the vampire king. It sounds too crazy to be true, no matter how hard you try to suspend your disbelief.

"Yes, the one and the same," I chuckle.

"Why are you there?"

"Let's just say we have a deal, and if he dies, I don't get my money," I opt for this explanation. Telling him that I don't want Hannibal to die because I've fallen madly in love with him and I have no idea how I'm ever going to imagine my life without him seems like the wrong choice, which I shall keep to myself.

"I see," he says, although I doubt he sees much, other than what I tell him.

"So, can you come here to the building and bring me those papers?" I ask.

"Like... right now?"

"What time is better than now, Quinn?" I wonder.

"What about my money?"

I sigh. "You want cash?"

"Yes," he says clearly.

"OK," I frown. "I'll have cash for you in an hour. Can you come then?"

"Sure thing," he nods. "Just send me the address."

"OK," I sigh.

Just as I'm hanging up the phone, Hannibal knocks on the door. I invite him in, wondering why he's standing in the doorway, instead of coming inside.

"Sorry to interrupt," he says, as if he's really interrupting something. "I need to jump to the office quickly. Will you be OK here?"

"Sure," I smile, nodding. "I'm not a baby, you know."

"I know," he echoes, his brows furrowing, as if there's a dark cloud appearing just above his head. "You know perfectly well why I'm asking this. You're prone to create trouble. I'm asking if you can stay out of trouble for the next hour, while you're alone at the apartment."

"Of course, I can," I smile, fluttering my long eyelashes at him.

"Aha," he replies, suspecting something obviously. But he doesn't know what to accuse me of. He doesn't know anything about my phone call, nor the fact that I need to leave this building to get some cold, hard cash, like Quinn requested.

"I'll be fine, relax," I urge. "Besides, do you really think that Plyn will let me out of his sight if I dare take one step out of the apartment? Come on."

This seems to pacify him. "I won't be gone long."

"I'll be fine," I reply. He waves, then a minute later, I hear the front door open, then close.

I jump from the bed and head in the same direction, grabbing my purse on the way. I know there is an ATM across the street. Only, the problem is that I can only withdraw as much as one thousand dollars per day. I have no idea how this will work, but I have to try. I have to speak to Plyn. I have to explain what I'm doing, and that it's all so we can find out who attacked Hannibal. Hopefully, he will understand.

I wait about fifteen minutes longer, then I head downstairs, finding Plyn in the same place as he was last time I was about to go out. He immediately notices me.

"I hope you don't think you're going anywhere," he warns me.

"I know I messed up," I say, lifting my hands in the level of my chest, in a gesture of surrender. "I just need to do something, out of the building. Come with me if you want. But it's very important."

"I'll be the judge of that," he corrects me.

I inhale deeply, going over everything that I've done, why I did it, and also everything that Quinn told me, in addition to the fact that he wants money for the info.

"Cold, hard cash?" Plyn repeats.

"Mhm."

"Who pays informants via bank transfer?" he almost laughs aloud. I feel a little awkward, but then I realize that it's OK. Something is telling me that he's on my side.

"I can only get one thousand," I add.

"How much more do you need?" he asks.

"Four."

"I can get you four," he says calmly. It is me who is unable to control the outburst of joy.

"Really?" I clap my hands together. He just nods.

"But this better be exactly what you told me," he warns. "Otherwise..."

"I know," I nod. "I can understand your suspicion. But trust me, I'm doing all this because I think whoever attacked Hannibal is also working against him at the company. Maybe if we dig a little more in the company papers, we might find out who this person is."

"Alright," he nods.

It takes us about half an hour to get five grand and fit it into my purse. Apparently, Plyn has a bank account that allows larger withdrawals. Meaning, we had the money. Now all we needed to do was exchange it for the documents. We go back to the foyer of the building, and we wait there. I keep checking my watch. It's been one hour and ten minutes. I'm on the verge of calling Quinn, to see if he's on the way, but I guess I should take into account traffic and other unforeseen circumstances.

Finally, we see him approaching the building. Plyn lets him in. Quinn gives him a puzzled look, but I clarify the situation.

"This is a friend, relax," I tell him. "I know you always said that it's just you and me meeting up every time, but I can't leave the building."

"Is it because of the Reyes contract?" Quinn asks. I nod. "But you do know he found someone else?"

"This seems to be a public secret now," I frown. "I thought it was supposed to be a proper secret. I mean, he's hiring someone to kill off a clan leader. That shouldn't be announced everywhere."

"You know that word travels fast," Quinn reminds me. "Besides, none of us want to get involved in any clan wars. If someone were to warn the leader, hey... they'll warn him. But it sure as hell won't be me. Now, if you'll just give me my money, so I can gracefully disappear from this hellhole, and never come back again... I'd really appreciate that."

"Not so fast," Plyn stands between us, as if to protect me, just in case Quinn decides to go rogue.

That is, of course, impossible. Quinn doesn't have that in him. He's a coward. But I guess exactly because he is a coward, he is usually not to be trusted. Despite this, I've come to trust him in the years that we've established this informant relationship, but still, I'm happy to be bringing it to an end.

"The documents first," Plyn instructs, putting out his hand.

Quinn looks at me, then at him. Obviously, he realizes he is left with no choice other than to comply. We make the exchange, and I quickly go over the papers in my hand. They make very little sense to me, but hopefully, when we show them to Hannibal, he'll know what to do.

"That's that then?" Quinn suddenly says, almost as if he doesn't really want to go, to call it an end.

"Yes," I nod. "I hope that money gets you everything you've ever dreamed of."

Quinn nods, placing the envelope inside his coat pocket, then heads out the door without another word. Before he opens the door, he turns around, waves quickly, and a moment later, he's gone. Plyn and I are left alone.

"I'll give you that money back," I assure him.

"That's fine," he sounds surprisingly understanding, almost as if we've become friends in the course of this conspiracy.

"Let's go back upstairs, so we can wait for Hannibal to come back."

He nods to my suggestion, and we both head for the elevators.

"You won't run this time, will you?" he grins as we're waiting for it to come.

I chuckle in response, staring him in the eyes. "Cross my heart and hope to die."

He smiles back.

Yes, maybe not friends, but hopefully, on the way there.

Chapter Twenty

Hannibal

I return to the apartment, with Irina and Plyn waiting for me in the living room.

"Hey, guys..." I greet them first, immediately realizing that there's obviously something they want to discuss with me.

At first, I think that Irina tried to go out on her own again. Plyn looks displeased, but not angry. So, maybe it's not that.

"We have something to show you," she tells me. "Why don't you sit down?"

Still curious as to what all this could be about, I do as she tells me. I sit down in the armchair that faces the sofa, waiting for the big reveal.

"Maybe you know this already," she continues, sounding a bit hesitant, "but we found out that someone's been stealing from your company. A lot."

I frown. I was expecting many things, but not this.

"What are you talking about?" I ask.

"This," she gives me a small folder. I take it, then open it.

I quickly skim through the papers. They all look like they're connected to my company, and all of them have one thing in common: there is a constant outflux of money. Way too much of it.

"I've seen some of these numbers," I tell her, lifting my gaze from the papers. "My financial department is led by a very competent man. I doubt he wouldn't notice that someone's been stealing right from under my nose."

But the moment I say that, I realize how naïve it sounds. Of course, it's possible, if he was bribed into turning a blind eye to all of this. You can make anything happen if you have a lot of money and you offer it to the right people.

There is only a small percentage of people who are not tempted by any amount. It is those people you want to find in this world and keep them close to you. But they are rarer than hen's teeth.

"I thought the loss of all this money was just the result of some bad business decisions," I shrug. "Why would you think that someone's embezzling money?"

Irina jumps up from her seat and comes over to me. The sweet fragrance of her perfume immediately hits my nostrils. It both calms me down and thrills me at the same time. But I have to focus on the conversation we're having. If they are right, then we have a rat in the company. This makes me angry. Mostly with myself, because I was sure that I can always smell a rat.

"There are numerous mentions of this one, small company," she points out, grabbing the papers from my hand and skimming through them, until she manages to find exactly what she is looking for. "Here," she points with her elongated finger.

I look at what she is pointing. Asmodeus Co.

Suddenly, it sounds familiar. But... it can't be.

Without telling them anything, I jump up and rush to my study. I pull the drawer to the desk open, rummaging through the top papers, although I know it's not at the top, but somewhere buried deep inside. It's been a while since I authorized that document and just shoved it into the drawer, not needing to think about it again.

"What are you looking for?" I hear Irina ask, as she's standing by the door.

"I know that company," I tell her hastily, still focused on the task at hand.

"Do you know who owns it?" she asks, her voice trembling.

I don't answer that. I still don't want to believe it. But with that name... I doubt I'm mistaken. I thought it sounded familiar. Perhaps, it could still be something different. It could be a whole other company, belonging to someone else.

I keep going through the papers, throwing them onto the ground carelessly. This isn't who I am. I usually keep everything in meticulous order, but right now, order is the last thing on my mind. I just want to find that damn document so I can prove to myself that it's not him.

Irina is just standing there, waiting. With the corner of my eyes, I notice that Plyn is there, behind her as well.

"How did you find this?" I ask, while still looking.

I need them to focus on something else, rather than just staring at me being a slob, throwing my documents all around the room, while trying to find that one.

"I have my sources," she shrugs.

I lift my gaze at her, frowning. But I'm not looking at her, I'm looking at Plyn.

"Did she go out again alone?" I ask him.

"No," he assures me. "I went with her. Then the guy came here, to bring us that."

I don't say anything, but I'm relieved that we didn't have the same episode repeat itself. The truth is, I don't know what I'd do if Irina got hurt. Especially, while I was supposed to protect her. I doubt I would ever be able to forgive myself.

"So, what are you thinking Hannibal?" I hear her ask. She isn't ordering. She is pleading.

But... I can't share what's on my mind. I just can't. Not yet. Not until I am fully convinced that I'm right in thinking so.

A moment later, I have what I'm looking for right in my hands. It's a cluster of a few papers, clipped together. I quickly skim through all of them, finally reaching the last one, where we all signed our names.

I rake my fingers through my hair nervously. My eyesight becomes foggy. The signature right in front of my face starts to dance around, mocking me.

"There," I give her the document, as if the mere presence of it in my hands burns my skin.

The truth is, it doesn't burn my skin, but rather, my very soul. I slump down into the chair, not minding the mess that I've created in the process of finding this.

Irina takes a look. I can see her eyes widening in shock. She turns to Plyn and shows it to him as well. Plyn looks at me somehow sorrowfully. I know he wasn't expecting it either. You never expect it to be those who are closest to you, those who have access to every part of your mind and soul, those who know absolutely everything about you.

"Hannibal..." Irina says my name, but then, doesn't know how to continue.

I understand that feeling. She wants to say she's sorry. But there's nothing to be sorry about, except for the fact that sometimes, we are too stupid to see something that's right in front of our noses.

"What do you want to do?" Plyn asks a more practical question, and I appreciate it as much as Irina's concern.

I need both right now. I need loving care and concern, as well as practical guidance into solving this matter as quickly and as painlessly as possible. Although, I doubt that will be doable. You can't stab someone in the back, and then expect them not to be hurt, not to be in horrible pain after finding out. Then again, it's obvious that you were wrong about everything regarding this person. And this hurts the most.

"We're going to see him, of course," I tell Plyn. "Right now."

"Should I call Mortar?" he asks.

"No," I shake my head. "It will be just you and I, old friend."

Irina frowns at this. "You don't think I'm staying behind, do you?" She sounds like an offended child and, strangely, I just want to pinch her cheek for this.

"You're not going," I order. "I can't focus on him and keep an eye out on you at the same time."

"You seem to be forgetting who you're talking to." Her eyes flare up at the insinuation that she can't take care of herself.

Just one look at her and I know she won't do as I told her. She won't stay here a moment longer, after Plyn and I leave. So, I guess there is no point in trying.

"Fine," I sigh. "You can come."

"I will come," she corrects me. "I don't need your permission."

She sounds a little offended still, so I try to clarify. "Listen... I didn't mean that you can't take care of yourself. I know you can. I know who you are. Why do you think I chose you of all the other women in the whole city?" I pause. She seems to like hearing that. "But... I'm worried. That's all."

She places her hand on my cheek, caressing me gently. "Let me come."

Her choice of words surprises me. Now, she is asking for my permission. Sometimes, you just can't win with these women, especially with women like Irina. And I wouldn't have it any other way.

"Just don't get hurt, OK?" I advise, with a smile.

"You bet," she smiles back, leaning close to me and giving me a peck on the lips.

This seems so intimate, so personal, that it makes my knees weak. No other woman has ever managed to do that. Not even Xeena. She was brave, but I can't imagine her ever demanding to come with me into a situation such as this one. Irina didn't even blink. She demanded to come. She wouldn't have agreed to any other option. That is the kind of woman for me. One who can make up her own mind, even if it's a decision I may not like at first. A woman with a strong head on her shoulders. A real queen fit for a real king.

I see now why I've been pining so long for Xeena. The reason is simple. I had no idea that someone better, someone more worthy would eventually come along, and I would lose my all to her.

I don't know what will happen when we return. Perhaps everything will remain the same. Perhaps everything will turn upside down. But I want to come along for the ride. I want to open myself up again. I want to allow myself to feel. I guess I've been feeling all this time, I just pretended that I wasn't. One look at Irina has always been enough to create a storm of emotion inside of me. And I know that I want her by my side forever. For better and worse, in sickness and in health. In times of peace, as well as war.

These are times of war, and she is my warrior queen.

Chapter Twenty-One

Irina

I have no idea what Hannibal's plan could possibly be. It's just the three of us going to Everild's home, to demand explanations. It sounds like child's play, not a matter of life and death.

I mean, what can we do, just the three of us? Threaten him? Frighten him? Hurt him? It's laughable. He's probably surrounded by a million bodyguards. They'll blow us away like candles on a birthday cake. But I don't say anything. Hannibal knows, and that's good enough for me.

We arrive to a big country house on the outskirts of the city. The guards let our car pass easily as soon as they see Hannibal. Hopefully, that'll give us the element of surprise, but we're still severely outnumbered.

We park the car right in front of the classical antebellum house, with huge pillars and a balcony that stretches all the way from one side of the house to the other, creating a wide porch right at the very entrance. When we get out of the car, only then do I notice that grand garden with perfectly upkept shrubbery, which seems to be in perfect symmetry with the house.

We are welcomed by someone who greets Hannibal very cordially, then turns his attention to Plyn and me. Before he does that, Plyn leans over to me whispering. "That's Everild's right hand man."

In other words, that is the guy we need to take out first, when shit hits the fan.

We enter the house, which is even more lavish on the inside than on the outside. There is an enormous foyer which leads into a sweeping, open staircase. The walls are decorated by intricate shapes and patterns, and there are large mirrors everywhere.

It is then that Everild makes his theatrical appearance, coming down the staircase, almost like a belle of the ball, coming down before her suitors.

"Ah, guests!" he exclaims, sounding happy to see us. He comes down and greets us all. "I thought I was meeting up with you at your place," he tells Hannibal.

"A change of plan," Hannibal smiles. "There is this urgent little business that I... I mean, we need to discuss with you... in private," he adds the last part, glancing at the few thugs standing about, looking like they have nothing better to do than just stand around.

Everild seems a bit surprised, but he is still smiling. "Of course," he nods. "We could go to my office." He turns around, and starts walking, so we follow closely behind. Hannibal is right by his side, while Plyn and I walk like a pair as well. I hear footsteps behind me, but I don't turn around. It's probably Everild's right hand man, just keeping a close eye on things.

We enter Everild's office, which is just as elaborate and intricate as the rest of the house, and at this point, it's all a bit too much. He sits down at the big, oak desk, Hannibal takes a seat opposite him, while Plyn and I find our place on a leather sofa in the corner of the room, overseeing them as well as the door.

Plyn looks in the same direction, and I know what he's thinking. If someone enters, we'll be able to jump on them, immediately closing the door. This way, we might actually have a chance at getting out alive.

"So, what's up?" Everild asks, sounding curious.

Hannibal takes out the folded papers from inside his blazer pocket, places it on the table and slides it over to him. Everild looks at him, then down at the papers. He takes them into his hand and starts going through them quickly. With each passing word that he reads silently, his facial expression changes, until there is nothing left of the initial, welcoming smile. Only shock, disbelief, astonishment.

"Care to explain this?" Hannibal asks calmly.

I can't help but admire him at that moment. I would be screaming at this guy. This is my best friend, who decided it would be ok to stab me in the back. Worst of all, this might be connected to the fact that he hired someone to kill me. I would never be able to sit here, looking and sounding so calm. But that's Hannibal. He knows how to handle things. That is why he is the king.

Everild sighs heavily, putting the papers down. "I suppose it was bound to come up sooner or later."

Hannibal frowns. Plyn immediately leans a bit forward, as if he's half-ready to jump, if Hannibal is attacked. I place myself in a state of readiness immediately as well.

"How long have you been stealing money from me?" Hannibal asks.

"How long have you been stealing time, effort and my dreams?" Everild asks angrily.

The hairs on my arms immediately stand on end. I can feel the electricity in the air around us.

"What are you talking about?" Hannibal growls back. This time, there is no sign of serenity. It was just a calm before the storm.

Everild glares back at him. A fight is imminent. That much is obvious. But they need to clarify things first.

"Fuck, Hannibal," Everild's eyes turn into little slits on his face from all the glaring. "You're so conceited, you can't see what's right in front of your nose. I've been doing this for years, waiting to see when you'll notice. Look how long it took you."

I know how Hannibal feels about Everild. I can't imagine how he's just sitting there, listening to him, without reacting in some way. It must take much more effort to remain calm than to explode, that's for sure.

But I also know that Plyn and I are ready. I can see it in the way his body has tensed up, the way he's not taking his eyes off Everild and Hannibal, his eyes watching one, then the other, in a perpetual circle.

Hannibal pushes the chair behind him, standing up. So does Everild. Now they are standing, facing each other, like two raging bulls. The truth is out. At least, a part of it. Plyn and I jump up as well. Everild has to know that, as long as it's just the four of us here, he's outnumbered. But I'm sure that there's a button of some sort, somewhere on his desk, at an arm's reach. All he has to do is press it, and everyone will barge in through that door. There will be nothing we can do to stop them. There will be too many of them. We won't go down without a fight, I know that much as well.

"You've been stealing from me," Hannibal says angrily. I expect him to lunge at Everild now, but Hannibal is still keeping his distance, and Everild is still standing by the desk, unwilling to move. That safe button may be right by his side. I'm surprised that he hasn't pressed it yet. Maybe he thinks that he's got everything under control.

"You don't get it, do you?" Everild almost laughs at this point, and I want to wring his neck for treating Hannibal in this way. "I want everything you have. It was always supposed to be mine. But you thought you were better than me. You thought we were all here to serve you. All hail the almighty Hannibal Delacruz!" he is shouting at this point, mockingly bowing down before Hannibal, who is still surprisingly calm.

But I know that when he explodes, it will be one for the books.

"I thought you were my friend," Hannibal tells him. "I always considered you not only my best friend, but a brother."

"Thanks for that," Everild continues to mock him. "That allowed me to get close to you, to plan my revenge. Only... I should have hired more competent people to do the job. I should have known that you wouldn't be that easy to kill."

At that point, he reaches down underneath the desk, and obviously does something. By doing something we all assume that he's pressing that button. In no time, we'll be surrounded by his men.

"I should have known that if I wanted it done well, I would have to do it myself," Everild finally steps away from the desk, in a theatrical show of strength and determination.

I know that Hannibal could take him on, face to face. That much is obvious to all of us here. But Hannibal doesn't do anything. He's just staring at Everild. My only explanation of this is that he's fighting himself. He is fighting all the memories that he has with Everild, remembering everything they've been through, wondering how come Everild was ready to throw it all away for money and power. Those things truly make a person go wild, forgetting what truly matters in life.

"Do you really think you can kill me?" Hannibal suddenly asks.

Everild frowns. "What do you mean?" He's perplexed.

"Everyone knows I'm here," Hannibal says. That, I know, is a lie. Maybe Mortar knows. But he hasn't told anyone. "Do you really think you can kill all three of us here, take my company, my throne, and have it all done without any consequences?"

The question obviously confuses Everild, whose eyes widen in shock, revealing the thought process that must be going on inside his head. At that moment, the door bursts open, and just like I thought, several vampires barge in, looking vicious and ready to pounce.

Plyn and I stand our ground, moving closer to Hannibal. But it's obvious that we would barely be able to make a dent in their body armor.

"I can do whatever the hell I want," Everild hisses at Hannibal.

In a way, he's right. No one truly knows we're here. He could kill us, dispose of us, and maybe, some day, the truth might come out. But that's a big if.

"You seem to forget who I am," Hannibal growls back at him.

It is then that an explosion happens. I don't know who made the first blow. But I know that suddenly, everyone is involved. Hannibal is fighting Everild and winning. I can see that much through the rain of blows that I myself am handing out. The thugs around us are pouncing on us, and even though I never shy away from a fight, we are terribly outnumbered.

I take the first one down easily, by punching him in the stomach, twisting his arm backward so hard that I hear his shoulder snap, then I smack him with my fist against the jaw, leaving him unconscious on the ground. I take out the second one as well, with a little more effort. The third one, however, comes at me full on, with all of his energy, while mine is already dwindling. Plyn comes to my side, and that gives me some additional energy, to know that we're all still standing.

I keep throwing glances at Everild and Hannibal, who are still fighting. I notice that Everild is fighting dirty. I guess I should have known that. There were many things here that should have been known, that should have been anticipated, but we say that easily when remembering things in retrospect. When you're in the heat of the moment, all you can do is act and react. That is exactly what we are doing now.

While Hannibal is still fighting with his bare hands, Everild has pulled a knife, out of nowhere. I knew we were supposed to have come armed, but that isn't how Hannibal would have done it. I know it. He would have decided against it even if I had suggested it before heading here. Now I could surely use that Swiss army knife I always have on me in my backpack.

Slowly, I feel my strength leaving me. All I can hope is that the same thing isn't happening to Hannibal. But every time I look in his direction, I am assured that Everild has the upper hand, especially with that knife. The final time I turn around, I notice that blood is dripping down Hannibal's hand, and he is leaning to that side, as if he's losing balance.

Then, a sharp swirl of pain takes hold of me, and I can't remain standing on my feet any longer. I feel nausea coming on, realizing that one of the thugs must have punched me in my stomach. I lean forward, my hands pressed to my stomach.

A moment later, the guy falls down to the ground before me, and I realize that Plyn knocked him out.

"Thanks..." I manage to murmur, unable to breathe properly.

"You OK?" he asks, offering me his hand.

I nod, accepting it. "Hannibal..." I manage to say.

We both look in his direction, realizing he's on the ground and Everild is coming at him with a knife in his hand.

Chapter Twenty-Two

Hannibal

It's all become a haze. A mixture of anguish and blindness. I feel like my body isn't mine any longer. Everild knows my moves. He knows how to anticipate them. He's obviously studied my mode of fighting, getting himself ready for this moment.

Even as I'm in this position, lying almost unconscious on the floor, with numerous cuts on my body, leaking my life fluid, I still can't believe that all these cuts were made by someone I trusted, someone I never thought could do this to me.

It's becoming increasingly difficult to keep my eyes open. Sleep wants to take over me. But I can see that Everild is coming at me with that knife, which has already tasted my blood, and it wants more. It wants all of it. It wants to extinguish my life spark. Everild knew to bring a silver bladed knife. That is the only blade capable of killing a vampire.

He stands on top of me, looking down. He is grinning so happily, so wickedly. I always knew there was evil in this world. I knew this, and I tried to keep away from it. I tried to distill justice, although sometimes, justice tends to be cruel. It was the life I chose for myself. The position I climbed onto. But when you reach these heights, you're bound to make some enemies. You just don't think your friends will become your enemies.

He lowers himself down to his knees, spreading them around my body, keeping me pinned down. I could barely move even if I tried to.

"What a sad, pathetic fall for the king of vampires," Everild grins at me.

I don't want his grin to be the last thing I see. I try to move, but I can't. He's keeping me firmly down. I feel my strength slowly oozing out of my body. I'm lingering on the edge between life and death. The cuts from that silver blade have weakened me into passivity. That's exactly what he wanted.

He wanted to see me weak. He wanted to see me suffer, to see me down, unable to do anything, while he's standing on top of me, proving his power over me.

I use all my leftover strength to try and get him off of me, but it's all in vain. I barely manage to move myself, let alone him. All the while, he's still grinning, those horrible white fangs protruding from his mouth.

He takes the knife in both of his hands, then lifts it above his head. I can see the crazy look in his eyes. This is what he's been planning on doing all along. Nothing will stop him. These are my last moments alive.

I don't regret a single thing in life. Maybe, mourning my relationship with Xeena for so long. Or not having met Irina sooner. But nothing else.

I turn to the side, to see where she is. And that is when I see her. She is running behind Everild. He can't even see her. Just before he's about to stab me with the knife, she jumps on his back, pulling him off of me.

I lift my head to see what's happening. They're rolling around. One moment, she's the one on top, the next moment, it's him. Instantly, the knife flashes, then disappears. My eyes widen in shock when I see that Everild pulls his hands away, devoid of any knife in them.

I use all my strength to get up. I see Irina lying on the floor, with the knife deep in her belly. Everild turns to me. I can see from the evil glimmer in his eyes what he wants to do.

He bends down and pulls the knife out of her. He looks at me, bringing the blade to his mouth, then licking the blood off of it. Something inside of me snaps. The last remnants of my energy rise to the surface, and I try to get up, but Everild kicks me in the stomach, and I fall back down.

"First I'm going to finish your girlfriend," he tells me. "But you'll watch. She will die because of you. Then, I'm going to finish you and a new reign will start."

He turns to Irina again, and I know he'll kill her if I don't do something. Forgetting about all the pain that is surging through my veins, through my entire body, I lunge at Everild just like Irina did. I start pounding on him, my fists like machines, finding the bull's eye of his face, landing blows as if my life depended on it, because it does. My life depends on it. More importantly, Irina's life depends on it.

I don't know how long I keep hitting him, and every blow hurts me as much as it hurts him, but I can't stop. I know if I stop, it might be too late to start again. All could be lost. I have to keep going, until there isn't even a single ounce of energy left in me.

I don't even know what I'm doing any longer. I feel like some strange force has taken me over, and I am just watching it from the sidelines, completely separated from my own body. I feel like I am punishing Everild with every blow for what he has done to me, to us, to Irina. I doubt I will ever be able to forgive him. What's worse, I doubt I will ever be able to trust someone like that again. It's so sad, because I still have people who are counting on me, people who love me, people who would give their lives for me.

I have seen that. Irina jumped onto his back, taking that knife stab into herself, when it was aimed at me first. She never hesitated. She wanted to save me, even at the cost of killing herself.

That thought fills me with even more rage, and my punches become even more uncontrolled, even more furious, and I know that if I keep doing this, I might kill him. But not a single part of me cares about this, because he didn't care one bit when he pushed that knife into Irina's delicate body, which was now lingering on the brink of life and death.

Suddenly, Plyn pulls me away, and I realize that Everild is unconscious. I can't even tell if he's breathing. But I don't care. I quickly turn to Irina. Her hands are pressing on the wound in her stomach, and there is a thin trickle of blood running down the corner of her mouth. I rush over to her, knowing that there is only one thing that can save her now.

"Irina?" I call out to her. "Can you hear me?"

I place my hand underneath her head, like a pillow, propping her up. She manages to look at me, although I can see that she's holding on with the last morsels of energy. That should be enough.

"Does it hurt?" I ask.

She frowns, rolling her eyes. Then, she nods.

"That's my girl," I press the other hand to her cheek. "Listen to me now. I have to do something to you now, something that will save you, but it will feel like someone is tearing you apart, limb from limb. Do you understand?"

She is still frowning. I'm not sure if she even hears me properly, but I have to explain to her how this functions. She's known enough vampires to be well aware of the whole process of becoming a vampire. It doesn't happen as easily as humans think. It's fucking painful. It feels like you're dying. In a way, you are dying, only to be reborn again, in a slightly different form. But for this to happen, your old self needs to die first, and no death is a pleasant process.

"It will hurt, Irina," I repeat. "A lot. But you have to bear with me, OK?"

Trembling, she nods.

I look up at Plyn. I know what he's thinking. Irina is on the brink of death. Biting someone in that condition might have the adverse effect. It might kill them more quickly.

I see that wound. It's too deep. We might be able to stop the bleeding for now, but I know that we wouldn't be able to reach any hospital in time. She would die on the way there. I can't allow that to happen. I promised I would keep her safe. I promised that nothing would happen to her. I promised her that she would be able to start a new life, the life she always wanted... only I want that new life to include me in it.

"I have to do this," I whisper to Plyn. He nods, understanding.

I wrap my arms around her, bringing her closer to me. She feels as light as a feather, her body seems to have almost shrunk with all that lack of blood. It feels like her soul is leaving her body right in front of me, and I fear there might be nothing I can do about it.

"Stay with me, my love," I whisper into her ear. "Don't leave me."

I have no idea if she can hear me or not at this point. Her eyes are closed. I look at her chest. There is still an indication of breathing. She is still with us. But I fear it might not be for much longer.

I take one of her hands and bring it to my lips. It is already much paler than usual. I glance at her stomach. Some of the blood has crusted, but there is still some of it that is bright red, meaning that the bleeding hasn't stopped. I have to do it immediately. I can't wait a moment longer. Time is of the essence here.

My own hand trembles as I bring her wrist all the way to my lips. I hesitate for one last moment, before digging my teeth into her wrist. Hot, red blood immediately spurts out, and I suck every bit of that precious blood into me, feeling it revive me.

I keep her body close to mine, hugging her, not letting her go, just like I promised. Whatever happens, I want it to happen to us together, with her in my arms...

Chapter Twenty-Three

Irina

At first, the pain becomes unbearable. When that bastard stabs me with the knife, it feels like I died instantly. The pain is too much to handle, like an explosion of heat in my stomach, as if someone pressed hot coals right onto my bare skin. Then, as moments pass by, my mind gets used to the sensation, controlling the onslaught of pain. I manage it somehow. I keep reminding myself that I'm fine. It's nothing to worry about. I'll stop the bleeding.

I even manage to press my hands to my belly, not paying attention to the wet feeling, as if someone left the faucet open and the water was just trickling without stopping. I try not to pay any attention to that, keeping fear under control.

Then, Hannibal slumps down onto the ground next to me. I'm happy to see that he's alive, but I can barely smile at him through the pain. I can barely keep my eyes open. I feel so tired, I just want to let go, close my eyes and go to sleep.

But I know what that would mean. Sleeping would mean giving up. It would mean that I was letting go of life, when I wasn't ready to do that yet. I had too many plans. I had a new life to start. I had too many things to admit to this asshole who now had his arms around me and was telling me that he's gonna cause me more pain.

More pain? My mind keeps rewinding this sentence, wondering what he had in mind.

Then, the moment he digs his teeth into my wrist, I immediately realize. He wants to turn me into a vampire, so I could survive. Only... I might not. It all depends on how serious the wound is.

As soon as I feel his teeth in my wrist, more pain explodes all throughout my body. Now, it feels even worse. This is like being stabbed by that same knife over and over again, in every other part of my body. I start to twitch, but I can still feel his arm around me, keeping me close, as if he doesn't want to let go of me. That gives me strength to go through this horrible ordeal.

I can't even keep my eyes open anymore. It is all too much. My body is exhausted. My mind finally lets go, and everything turns black.

WHEN I OPEN MY EYES again, I realize that I'm in bed. I'm in my bed, in Hannibal's apartment. I look down at my hands. My left wrist is bound with a gauze. There is a faint flicker of red. Just a reminder of what happened, of what I survived.

I lift my head. I'm still dizzy. But I don't want to lie down any longer. I want to see Hannibal. I want to make sure he's alright. I want to see if Plyn is alright, too. Slowly, I focus on getting out of bed. I pull the cover from my body, and only this one action reminds me of the amount of pain my body is in. I have to take it slow.

I inhale deeply, putting one foot down, then the other. Now, for the more difficult part. I actually have to get up. I use my hands to lift myself up and manage to do it.

Walking turns out to be more difficult than I expected it. I creep along walls, using them to keep myself up, standing. I manage to come only to the hallway, when I hear Hannibal's voice.

"What are you doing out of bed?" he asks.

I turn around, only for our eyes to lock.

"Good grief, you look like shit," I tell him, watching his beautiful face all bruised and his lip cracked. Then again, I bet I don't look much better.

He chuckles at my comment. "I see you haven't lost your spunk," he notices. "That's a good thing."

"Right?" I smile.

He walks over to me and places my arm around his neck, so he can help me with balance.

"I'd kill for a coffee right now," I tell him.

"Let's get you one then," he nods, helping me to the kitchen, where he puts me gently down onto the chair. He proceeds to go and make coffee for both of us.

I can't keep my eyes off of him. My warrior. My brave king.

His arms are full of cuts. None of them are bleeding any longer, but some of the gashes look pretty deep and long, judging by the bandages. I look down at myself. Apart from my wrist and of course, my stomach, I can't really see much damage.

"My stomach..." I suddenly remember the stab wound I have.

I press my hand to my stomach, and there is still pain, but far from what I felt yesterday.

"Yesterday?" I ask aloud.

"What?" he chuckles. "Ask full questions, Irina. I can't read your mind."

"How long was I out?" I ask first.

"Two days," he tells me.

The coffee is ready shortly, and he pours us both a cup. The familiar smell immediately freshens me up, and I grab the cup with both my hands, disregarding the soft stinging sensation from the hot cup.

"Two days?" I wonder. "I was just... sleeping?"

"Yeah," he nods. "That's normal."

"Normal for becoming a vampire?"

"Mhm," he nods again, taking a sip. "For some, it's much longer than that. You took it like a champ."

"I did?" I chuckle at the comment.

"Absolutely," he nods. "I knew you'd do it easily."

"Even on the brink of death?" I remind him. "I know how it works. I could have died."

"You could have died either way. Take a look at your stomach," he gestures with his eyes.

I look down. Slowly, I grab the hem of my t-shirt with the tips of my fingers, lifting it up. It's bandaged up, so I can't really see how deep it is.

"If you were healing as a human, you wouldn't be able to breathe properly, let alone walk, talk and drink coffee," he points out. "But you're healing as a vampire now. That makes a whole lot of difference."

"Oh," I say, pressing the bandage gently with the tips of my fingers. There is pain, of course, but it's definitely not as bad as before.

In fact, I feel like I'm not really myself at this point, and I have no idea if it's because of the attack and the pain, or the fact that I'm no longer a human.

"You feel strange, don't you?" he asks, as if able to read my mind.

"How did you know?" I wonder.

"That's also another side-effect," he explains. "Almost as if someone placed you in a different body, and it feels a size too big, doesn't it?"

"That's exactly how I'm feeling," I nod, with a smile. "It's a feeling that will go away, won't it?"

"Of course," he assures me. "Everyone went through it, except for those who were born as vampires."

"Were you born a vampire?"

"Yes," he nods.

"Now, I'm a vampire, too," I point out, with a smirk.

"Yes," he chuckles.

"I have to ask you something," I suddenly say, looking a bit serious.

"Sure," he urges. "Anything." His eyes are focused on mine, drinking me in. I never want him to stop looking at me in this way.

"If I wasn't on the brink of death, would you ever make me into a vampire?" I ask.

He inhales deeply, somehow hesitant. "I feel like this is a trick question."

"Why?" I ask. "It's a simple yes or no question."

"Yes then," he finally says.

"Yes?" I echo.

"Yes," he chuckles. "How many yeses do you need to be sure of something?"

"Just one, I suppose," I smirk.

"But not then and there, of course," he clarifies.

"Of course," I nod. "At some other point."

"I feel like it's important to state here that I would want to do it, but the final say would be yours."

"Oh," I look at him, in an amused way. I feel like he's a bit awkward in this conversation, but I know where it is headed and what I want him to say. If he feels it, of course. "You'd ask me if I want to become a vampire?"

"I'd ask you if you wanted to become my queen," he finally says those words, and my heart feels like it's about to explode. I have to control myself, but it's getting more and more difficult with each passing moment, as he looks at me with those beautiful, loving eyes. The fact that we saved each other speaks more than any words ever could, but I still want him to say it. "Would you?" he asks loudly.

"I would," I say with a smile. "I will."

He gets up, walks around the table and takes me softly into his arms. He places his lips right onto my forehead, lingering there for a few moments, then pulls away, but still keeps his arms around me, as I lean with my back against the table.

"You know what this means, right?" he asks.

"What?" I tilt my head to look at him, as if that will help me understand exactly what he's referring to.

"I can't pay you," he finally says.

"What?" I snap, playfully punching his chest with my closed fist. It's just a gentle bump, without the slightest intention of hurting him. "Why on earth not?"

"Because now all my money is yours," he tells me. "You can do with it whatever you want. Buy a house, a plane, a bakery, an island. It's just money. I don't care about any of that."

"What do you care about?" I ask, blushing as I anticipate what his answer might be.

"You," he says exactly what I want him to say. "You are all I ever wanted. Luckily, I was smart enough to offer you that deal, because I doubt you'd have accepted my advances from the onset."

"You're right," I nod. "I wouldn't," I follow that with a shake of the head. "You had a smart strategy."

"See?" he chuckles. "I'm not the king for nothing."

"My king," I repeat, as I cup his face with my hands, bringing his lips to mine.

They taste sweet, even against the backdrop of pain and the lingering coppery taste of blood that we both can feel. But none of that matters, because we have the only thing that we ever wanted. We were just silly never to accept it, to admit it.

Perhaps even if we did, we wouldn't have found a way to each other. We were so stubborn that one of us needed to die and be reborn, in order for our love story to finally blossom.

When I pull away, I see the way he's looking at me.

"Did you just kiss me with your eyes open?" I wonder.

"Yes, why?" he chuckles.

"So, I could have opened them as well," I tease.

"Kiss me again and open them," he smiles.

"Wait," I pull my head away. "What about Plyn?" I ask.

"You want to kiss Plyn?" he teases playfully.

"No, silly," I punch him again on the chest as good-humoredly as last time. "Is he alright?"

"Of course," he nods. "He's a tough guy. You don't think they fall down so easily."

"No, but... it was a tough call at one point," I remember.

"It was," he agrees. "You proved yourself the bravest one."

"I wasn't," I shake my head. "I acted rashly. I wasn't thinking."

"Why weren't you thinking?"

"Do you really have to make me say it?" I blush again, even more than last time. That's so strange. He's the only man who has ever made me blush, the only man who ever had such a profound effect on me.

"I wasn't thinking because I..." I start, finding it somehow difficult to say those words. I never thought I would be saying them out loud, even though I feel like they've been residing inside of me for such a long time, trying to claw their way out.

"Because you...?" he urges me softly.

"Because I love you," I finally say it.

Strange. It seemed so scary a moment ago, but now that the words are out, I see there is nothing to be frightened about. They are just words. They are just emotions.

"I love you, too," he tells me, pressing his lips against mine once more.

This time, we're both keeping our eyes open, and instead of prolonging that kiss into something more passionate, we burst into loud laughter, pulling away.

The moment feels like pure perfection, and something tells me that this is what life will be with him. That is all I could ever hope for.

I rest my head on his shoulder, listening to the gentle sound of his heartbeat. I press my hand to his chest.

Mine, I think to myself. Mine.

Chapter Twenty-Four

Hannibal

A month passes by in a swirl. Irina fills my every day with more joy and happiness than I ever thought possible, sometimes with just her presence and nothing else. Some people are like that. They fill you with positive energy, they share their joy with you selflessly, making you a better person in the process. Because that's what I've become ever since she came into my life. A much better person. A person who's learned to leave the past in the past, and who can now focus fully on the present and the future.

Word of Everild's betrayal hit everyone almost as hard as it hit me. I wasn't expecting that. The council of leaders even got together, inviting me, to see whether everything was alright, whether I needed any help. The whole vampire community got together, showing me that one bad apple doesn't necessarily have to mean that the whole batch is rotten.

Irina's healing process was perfect. She has proven herself to be incredibly adaptive, and her wound was gone within a week. I've never seen anything like that, even with the toughest vampires out there.

That morning, she gets up from bed first. I turn to her side after a while, feeling her emptiness. I pat the space where she is supposed to be, but there's nothing. I open one eye, to peer if she's still in the room.

"Irina?" I whisper her name softly, but there is no response.

I lift my head. The bedroom is still dark. The curtains are drawn closed. She must have gotten up at some point and gone to another room. She usually sleeps in. So, I find this a bit strange, deciding to investigate.

I get up and walk over to the living room, but there is no trace of her. I check the kitchen, still nothing. Then, I find her sitting in my study, in my leather chair. She has her legs up, bent at the knee. She looks so small in that chair, as if some dark brown monster is about to eat her up.

"Hey, gorgeous," I call out to her, but she's already seen me and smiled upon my entrance. "What are you doing here all alone? Why aren't you in bed?"

She shrugs instead of a response at first. "I like this room."

"You like my study?" I wonder. "I never thought it was the nicest room in the whole apartment, but maybe you know something that I don't."

"This is where I broke your frame," she reminds me.

"Oh," I say. "I completely forgot about that."

It's the truth. Ever since I cleaned up that broken glass and removed the photo and the frame, I never once thought about them or remembered that it was there.

"You did?" she asks.

"Of course," I confirm. "You know everything about Xeena. I have nothing to hide. You also know that she means nothing to me now. She belongs to the past and that is where she will stay. You and I are the present."

"You don't have to be that convincing, I believe you," she chuckles.

"Well... I don't know why you'd remember her now," I shrug.

"Maybe because I'm thinking of additional people," she says, getting up from the chair, and walking over to me.

"Additional people" I frown. "What do you mean by that? What additional people?"

"You sound confused," she is still chuckling, obviously enjoying how confused she's making me.

"I am confused," I admit, but she eases my mind immediately as she approaches me and wraps her arms around my waist. I do the same to her, pulling her closer to me and kissing her forehead. "Do you want to shed some light on this mystery that seems to be so amusing to you, but is a cause of much distress for me, because I have no idea what you're talking about?"

She laughs aloud to this, and it is the sweetest sound ever. It is the only sound I want to listen to for the rest of our lives. A long time ago, I promised her that I would keep her safe. I almost failed in that promise. Now, I know that I will do anything not only to keep her safe, but to love her, cherish her, see that smile on her face every single day for the rest of our lives. And with vampires, that can be a helluva long time.

When she stops laughing, she looks at me straight in the eyes, almost as if she's expecting me to read the explanation in them.

"Are you happy?" she asks, even more cryptically now.

"Again... is this a trick question?" I wonder, shaking my head.

"No," she grins. "Just a yes or no question."

"Yes," I nod. "Then if it's really just a question regarding happiness, then yes. Absolutely. One hundred percent happy with you, as we are."

Suddenly, she frowns. "As we are?"

"Yes," I swear, I'm even more confused at this point. I have no idea what she wants to say, and I feel like I'm ruining it already, before she's even said it. "Or as we could be? Come on, I feel like I'm in the fryer here."

She chuckles. "OK, I've tortured you enough."

"That you have, and I plan on returning the favor," I assure her. "Now, spill it."

"I'm pregnant."

She says it so simply that, at first, I think I misheard her. Perhaps I'm just hearing what I want to hear. Perhaps she said something completely different.

"You're what?" I ask, just to be on the safe side, to see if I could explode with happiness this instant.

"Pregnant," she says that word again, and at that very moment, I grab her by the waist, lift her up into the air and start spinning her around.

She starts giggling like a schoolgirl, and once again, it is the most melodious sound that I've heard. I can already imagine how sweet our baby will be.

When I put her down, her cheeks are all flushed, and her eyes are sparkling in a way that they never did before. I have no idea how I didn't notice it before. She is glowing. She is so beautiful in that unearthly way that can only come from the realization that there is life growing inside of her.

"I can't believe it," I gasp, my mind still in a haze at the news.

"Are you happy now?" she asks, a little hesitant. "Because you said as we are..."

"Are you kidding me?" I ask, grabbing her by the cheeks and kissing the tip of her nose. "This is the best news you could have given me. I always wanted kids. So many kids. An infinite number of kids!"

"Whoa there, cowboy," she tells me with an amused chuckle. "Why don't we start with the first one, and then we'll see how many we can add."

"An infinite number of kids!" I repeat, lifting my hand up in the air victoriously.

She is still laughing.

"Tell me now, what can I make you for breakfast?" I ask.

"Oh, look at you, being all thoughtful," I hear her say. "And I'm not even properly pregnant."

I laugh at her comment. "What's properly pregnant?"

"When you can see the belly properly, silly," she explains, tightening the t-shirt around her thin waist. "See? You can't tell yet."

"Absolutely not," I shake my head at her flat belly. "But we know that there's a little bun in the oven."

I press my hand against her belly, already feeling an overwhelming love for this little being that I am yet to meet. I never thought that such things could bring so much joy. I realize that all this time, I've been focusing on the wrong things in life. But I suppose they weren't all that wrong, because they brought me to Irina. Or maybe they brought her to me. It doesn't really matter. What matters is that we are now together, bound by fate.

"Come," I take her by the hand, leading her to the kitchen. "I'm gonna feed you everything we have."

"What?" she is still smiling, unable to remove that feeling of sheer joy from her face. Then again, why would she want to? "You want me to be a fat preggo?"

"I want you to be the sweetest, most plump, fat preggo," I correct her, pinching her cheek, enjoying the look of sheer joy that she is exuding.

"Well, fat chance," she says, sticking out her tongue at me playfully. "I don't plan on being a fat preggo."

"Seriously?" I pout, faking being disappointed. "I was hoping to have a cute little muffin by my side."

"Nope," she shakes her head at me, caressing her belly. "We plan on eating healthy... with cheat days, but shhh, don't tell anyone!"

I press my finger to my lips. "Your secret is safe with me."

I stop when we enter the kitchen, just before she is about to sit at the table, and once again, I wrap my arms around her, unable to let go.

"What's up with you this morning?" she wonders, enjoying the physical affection.

"First, I missed you in bed," I explain. "Then, you told me that we're having a boy, and I'm– "

"Wait, what?" she laughs. "I never said we're having a boy. We're having a baby."

"I'm just joking," I wink at her, pinching her cheek playfully again. This morning is turning out to be so much fun. "I want a boy as much as I want a girl. We'll be having an infinite number of kids, after all."

"You're crazy," she shakes her head at me, rolling her eyes at the same time, all the while laughing. This is the sound that I always want to have in my home. And now, she will fill it not only with that, but also with the sound of children. There is nothing I ever wanted more than that.

"Crazy about you," I correct her again. "And about this little bundle of joy you're brewing for me. And it doesn't matter what kind of a preggo you are, fat, thin, big, small, I would still love you until the end of time."

"You sweet talker you," she says, wrapping her arms around my neck and pressing her lips against mine.

"I thought now that I have you, I had everything I could ever possibly need," I reveal. "But you managed to prove me wrong. You managed to prove that I did need someone else in my life, someone who will be a mixture of your beauty and my brain."

"What?" She punches me playfully on the shoulder. "How about my beauty, my brains and your brawn?" She suggests an alternative, which sounds even more amusing than my version, so I have to comply.

"That actually sounds great," I agree, finally letting her go from my arms, albeit reluctantly. "Now, what can I make you for breakfast?"

"I could get used to this special treatment," she comments, taking a seat at the table. "I would like some coffee, and boiled eggs on toast with some butter."

She keeps on listing all the stuff that she wants, and all I can do is nod. Because, what else can you do when you've got everything you could ever possibly need in life sitting right opposite you at the kitchen table?

Epilogue – Five Years Later

Irina

I close my eyes, feeling the soft breeze on my skin. The sun is burning bright, but not overly hot, although it's early afternoon. There is pleasant shade from the nearby trees, and I'm listening to the sound of splashing water.

I press my hand to my bulging belly. This is the second time around. I already know how it will go. I should be much less nervous, but I'm almost as nervous as I was with Rose.

The very thought of her makes me immediately open my eyes. I find her and Hannibal splashing in the lake. The joy on her face is immeasurable. He just knows how to deal with her. It is an absolute wonder to watch the two of them play. They have such similar characters. They are always out, looking for action, and he completely understands that need she has, because he shares it as well.

As for me, I have always been an introvert. I can only hope that this second baby will like books and being inside more than running after lizards and butterflies, and constantly wanting to be out and about, especially if it's raining.

I can't take my eyes off them. Although Rose has every single characteristic that Hannibal has, she is a spitting image of her mother. Everyone says so. I wonder what our second baby will look like. Just like with Rose, we decided to leave the gender a surprise. When I gave birth to Rose, we already had two names picked, so it was easy to call out her name as soon as we saw her. She was as red as a rose, with those sweet chubby cheeks. She was the most beautiful thing both of us had ever seen, and it was only natural that she be a rose. No other name would do, we both knew that.

At that point, I see Rose get out of the shallow waters and get back on shore. On her way back to me, she keeps bending down to pick flowers, and at one point, there is a whole bunch of them in her chubby little hand. She runs to me gaily, with those big brown eyes all excited and proud.

"Mommy! Mommy!" she shouts so loudly that it echoes all around us.

"What is it, sweetie?" I ask, opening my arms to welcome her.

She slumps down onto the picnic blanket next to me, careful with my belly, while I embrace her.

"This is for you," she tells me, offering me the bouquet of flowers.

"For me?" I gush. "Thank you, sweetie. They are absolutely precious."

I lean over to kiss her, feeling her wet feet and legs on mine.

"Is daddy coming out of the lake?" I ask, looking over her shoulder, but I see him lowering himself all the way into the water, then rising out and walking over to us. As soon as he nears us, I warn him. "You better not plan on stepping one wet foot on this blanket, mister."

Rose chuckles. She always likes it when I call him mister. She says daddy isn't a mister. He is a king. Sometimes, even little kids know before adults do.

"And here I was, just thinking of doing that very same thing," he says with a mischievous grin. "Besides, you're not the boss of this blanket. Rose is." He turns his attention to Rose, and hearing her be the boss of something, immediately makes her sit upright and look all important. "So, little miss Rose, do I have your permission to step my wet foot onto this picnic blanket?"

Rose chuckles again, her cheeks blushing at being addressed so importantly. She looks up at me, as if she's looking for guidance. I gently smile at her.

"It's your decision, sweetie," I urge. "Can daddy come wet on the blanket?"

"Well..." she suddenly seems to ponder, pressing her little index finger to her chin, which almost makes me chuckle out loud, but I don't want to make her feel self-conscious. "Daddy is a king, and kings can do whatever they want."

Hannibal immediately latches onto this. "I like this reasoning!"

I send him a scolding look, but it's all in good fun.

"So, I say daddy is allowed!" Rose announces, and Hannibal jumps between us on the blanket, making us both wet as he wraps us in his big, bear hug.

"Daddy! You're all wet!" Rose whines, trying to wiggle free out of his embrace.

"What?" Hannibal asks, as he starts tickling her. "You said daddy is the king, and kings can do whatever they want. Right now, I want to tickle a little Rose!"

With those words, he starts tickling her belly, which makes Rose drop onto her back with her legs up in the air, like a little beetle who turned over, and is now unable to get back up to her feet.

Once the tickle session is finished, Rose remains on the blanket, in a lying position. She adjusts her head on my thigh, as I caress her hair. I can tell that she is exhausted. Just as I thought, a few peaceful minutes later, her eyes are closed and there is only the sound of rhythmical breathing.

"You exhausted the baby," I tell Hannibal, gesturing at our slumbering Rose.

"You mean the sleeping beauty?" he corrects me. "She hates being referred to as a baby. She says she is a big girl now."

I laugh. "She can say whatever she wants. She will always be my baby."

"And you will always be mine," he leans in and kisses me on the cheek.

I smile at him, enjoying the moment. Everything is pure perfection. From the nature around us, the fresh air, the sound of Rose asleep between us to the love that Hannibal has for me, which never seems to diminish, but only grows with each passing day. I have no idea what I did to deserve this wonderful man by my side, but I'm not the one to be questioning fate.

After the ordeal with Everild, life pretty much went back to normal, but I've noticed that Hannibal was reluctant to open up to people again. He kept to his closed circle and that was that. I could understand that. He was almost killed by his best friend, the person he trusted more than anyone else. That is a traumatic experience, and it takes a long time for someone to heal after something like that.

That is why me, Plyn and Mortar did all we could to ease this process for him. We never pushed him to do anything he wasn't comfortable with. We allowed him to do everything in his own pace. But being the king meant that he couldn't remain locked off from the rest of the world, no matter how much he would like to be. Other vampires would not understand that. They would not accept it.

Fortunately, in the beginning, they had compassion for him, especially the circle of the elders and all the other clan leaders. They offered help, support, whatever he needed, although he told them that he needed nothing. It was simply his way of coping with what happened.

He remained closed off. His company wasn't as lucrative as before. He lost a lot of money, and that had nothing to do with any shady business. He was simply disinterested in it. Then, slowly, it started to change. He was slowly finding his faith in other people again, in other vampires.

It took him a while, but he started to let others into his life again, to meet new people and give them a chance to prove themselves worthy of his trust and his friendship. Of course, one always has to be cautious with others, but one also cannot be a solitary creature. It is simply not how we are wired, and I think he realized that eventually.

"You make me so happy," I suddenly hear him say, his voice breaking the magic of the silent moment.

"You make me happy as well," I smile back at him.

"No..." he shakes his head, and for a moment, I feel like something gripped the inside of my stomach, twisting it in anticipation of what he's about to say. Then, he continues, while I'm listening to his words, to his voice, intently. "I know everyone says this. You make me so happy. But... I feel it like the only truth in my life. I feel like I haven't known real happiness before I met you. I mean, of course, I was happy about certain things, I was glad. I can't deny that. But this feeling..."

At that point, he presses his hand to his chest.

"This feeling," he continues, and his every word fills my heart with more love than I ever thought I could possibly handle, "is the best feeling in the whole world. I don't know how else to describe it. It is also a feeling that no one else has made me feel but you, Rose," he pauses to caress Rose's perky cheeks, and then his hand travels to my belly, "and this new baby. You are all I ever wanted, and if I had to, I would give everything I own, everything I ever had, just to keep you. Because I need nothing else but you."

"Hannibal..." I whisper his name lovingly, overwhelmed by his words. "That was wonderful." I caress his cheeks, and he lowers his forehead to mine. We remain like that for a long time, neither of us saying anything.

After all, there is nothing to say. What words can you use when the emotions you have cannot possibly be expressed in any words? They can only be felt with all of your heart, not half of it or only with some of it. For this kind of love to happen, you have to truly open yourself up to not only love, but also to the possibility of heartache and pain. That is the only way. You risk it all. Only with the biggest risks can you obtain the biggest gains. We've both learned that.

We were both unable to fight this attraction we felt for each other. At first, that was all it was. Physical attraction. Jealousy that someone else was looking at him, wanting him. How that hostess undressed him with her gaze. I will never forget that.

When I told him how jealous I was of her, he told me that nothing ever happened between them. I believed him, of course. There was no need for him to lie. I was also glad that all she could do was fantasize about sleeping with him, while I had him by my side every single night. I had him next to me, inside of me. I had him in every single way. And he had me in return.

Then, this physical attraction gave way to love. First, it was just a flicker of a fire that we both tried hard to extinguish. We didn't believe it could bring anything good. We were both burned. Him much more than me, so I understood why he felt that way. I also never wanted to commit, especially not to him. It was ridiculous to even consider it a possibility.

And yet, it was much more than just a possibility. It was inevitable for me to fall for him, and to remain forever more, madly in love with Hannibal Delacruz. Because he is the kind of man, the kind of vampire, who once he knows who you truly are, he gives all of himself to you. He doesn't hold back. He will follow you to hell and back, to keep you safe.

I am the same. I died for him and was resurrected as I am now. Do I consider myself better as a vampire than a human? I don't know. I guess it doesn't matter. I would be his, in whatever shape or form I come, and I know that he would accept me and love me as I am. There is no doubt about it.

We both turn our gaze into the horizon, watching the sun set. The sky is painted in all the wonderful shades of red and orange. I lean my head onto his shoulder, inhaling his scent. I close my eyes. I don't need the beauty of that sunset any longer.

Not when I have something far more beautiful right in front of me.

I lean down to kiss Rose on the forehead. She stirs a little, then goes back to sleep. I rest my head again on Hannibal's shoulder, listening to the soft drumming of his heart that is forever mine, just like mine is forever his.

Enjoy what you read? Please leave a review!

Don't miss out!

Visit the website below and you can sign up to receive emails whenever Nikki Grey publishes a new book. There's no charge and no obligation.

https://books2read.com/r/B-A-TQTAB-BHHCF

BOOKS 2 READ

Connecting independent readers to independent writers.

Did you love *The Vampire's Search For A Queen*? Then you should read *Hunting The Vampire Prince*[1] by Nikki Grey!

[2]

It's my job to kill the vampire prince. But he saves me instead. My parents' jewelry store has gone bankrupt.Now we have to pay an enormous debt, or our whole family will be killed.My friend shows me how to be a bounty hunter – an easy way for someone like me who's skilled at fighting to earn money.When I take on the bounty on the fourth vampire prince of Romania I'm led to believe he's an evil man who murdered his brother and is plotting against the king.But what if he's actually a good person?What should I do about the attraction I feel towards him?I've never been intimate with a man.How am I supposed to kill the handsome gentleman who saves me from certain

1. https://books2read.com/u/4N7rQY
2. https://books2read.com/u/4N7rQY

death?Hunting The Vampire Prince is a standalone Paranormal Romance with a HEA and NO cheating!

Also by Nikki Grey

Hunted By The Vampire Prince
Hunting The Vampire Prince
The Vampire's Search For A Queen

Milton Keynes UK
Ingram Content Group UK Ltd.
UKHW042003281024
450365UK00003B/118